Take heed of the truths
that lie herein,
for they are the living legacy
of the Horadrim.

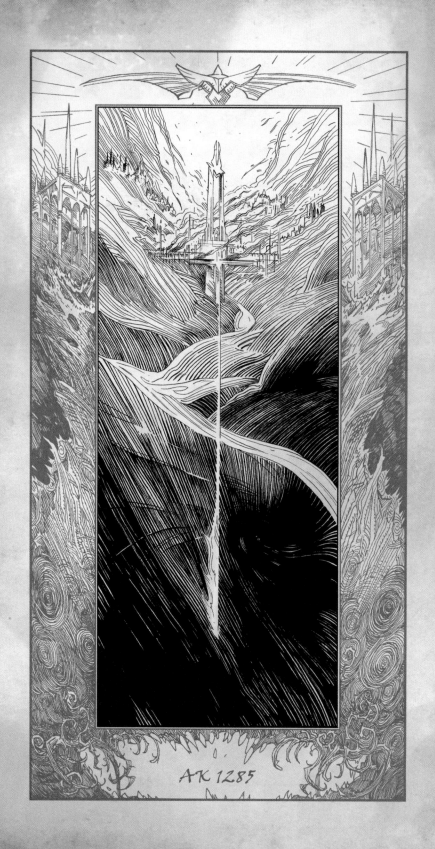

AK 1285

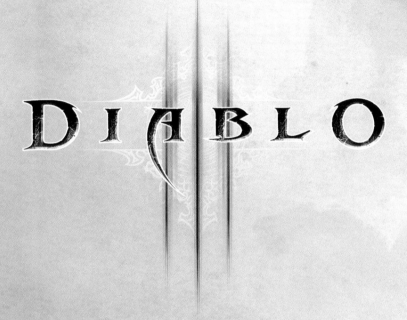

DIABLO III

BOOK OF TYRAEL

by Matt Burns and Doug Alexander

INSIGHT ◉ EDITIONS

San Rafael, California

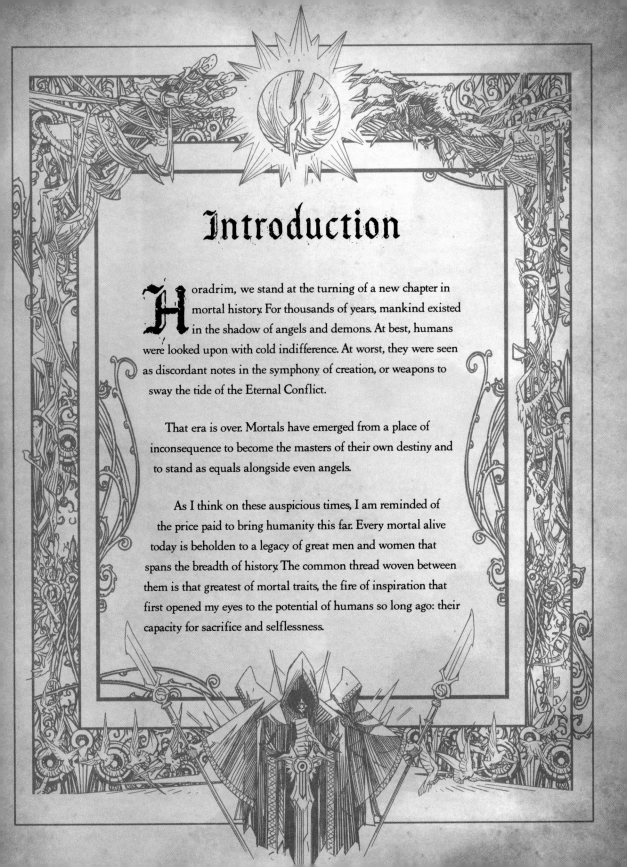

Introduction

Horadrim, we stand at the turning of a new chapter in mortal history. For thousands of years, mankind existed in the shadow of angels and demons. At best, humans were looked upon with cold indifference. At worst, they were seen as discordant notes in the symphony of creation, or weapons to sway the tide of the Eternal Conflict.

That era is over. Mortals have emerged from a place of inconsequence to become the masters of their own destiny and to stand as equals alongside even angels.

As I think on these auspicious times, I am reminded of the price paid to bring humanity this far. Every mortal alive today is beholden to a legacy of great men and women that spans the breadth of history. The common thread woven between them is that greatest of mortal traits, the fire of inspiration that first opened my eyes to the potential of humans so long ago: their capacity for sacrifice and selflessness.

I speak of Uldyssian ul-Diomed, the awakened nephalem. I speak of Tal Rasha and the first Horadrim; of the elderly scholar Deckard Cain, who carried on their teachings and beliefs. I speak of those brave individuals who vanquished the Prime Evil in the High Heavens, accomplishing a task that the angels themselves were unable to manage.

You know of them. You have read of their deeds and of the hard choices they made in the war to spare the hearts of mankind from evil. There is, however, another person who deserves recognition—someone who I fear that generations to come will misunderstand or even vilify.

Her name was Leah.

She was born to the witch Adria and the Dark Wanderer, a man whose body served as a vessel for Diablo, the Lord of Terror. From the moment of her birth, the demon's essence lurked within Leah, an unseen watcher hidden in the shadowed corners of her soul. When the time came, her own mother betrayed her, allowing Diablo to take hold of the young woman and twist her body into the Prime Evil reborn.

For some of you, this is everything you know of Leah. You may see her story as just another example of mankind's darker half and penchant for corruption.

But when I think of Leah, I do not see the face of evil. I see the niece of Deckard Cain, a kindhearted young woman who was the light of her uncle's life. I see a determined scholar hunched over stacks of ancient tomes, spending every waking hour searching for answers to forestall the coming End of Days. I see a friend, braving the legions of the Burning Hells, her hope an inspiration to everyone who fought by her side.

Leah never asked to take part in this struggle. The calling arrived unbidden, as it often does. Her uncle spent over twenty years of his life searching for a way to avert the End of Days. When death took him, his vast arcana—housed in dozens of books, research scrolls, and other vital items—were passed on to Leah, wrapped in the dying wish of the man who had been the only real family she had ever known:

It falls to you now, dear one, to draw your own conclusions
regarding these apocryphal texts—and to warn the world of the
perils that draw nearer with every passing day.

Those words, and the belief that humanity's future rested squarely on her shoulders, haunted Leah like a specter. She was not a scholar like Cain, nor was she a great mage like the first Horadrim. Nonetheless, she did not take the easy path and turn away from her calling. Instead, she devoted herself to it entirely. No matter how often she doubted herself, or how dark and winding her path became, she never looked back.

And she did all of this with Diablo's essence stirring in her heart.

Tal Rasha once said of mortals, "We cannot always change the future, but we can fight to guide it. In so doing, even if we fail, we will have set a path for others to follow."

I can find no better example of this wisdom than Leah. Even if she had known the truth of her origins—and perhaps near the end, she suspected it—it was beyond her ability to change. It was beyond any of our abilities to change.

So do not judge her based on what she became. Remember her, instead, as I do. See in her the great things that define all mortals: their innate ability to reach for heights unseen, to stand unyielding against an opposing force, to dream. Remember her as a worthy successor to all those whose sacrifices have brought us to this point in history.

I relate this to you because in the coming days, we would do well to find inspiration in Leah's story. Mortals have won many recent victories, but there is much to be done.

I refer you to the Prophecy of the End Days:

> *. . . And, at the End of Days, Wisdom shall be lost*
> *as Justice falls upon the world of men.*
> *Valor shall turn to Wrath—*
> *and all Hope will be swallowed by Despair.*
> *Death, at last, shall spread its wings over all—*
> *as Fate lies shattered forever.*

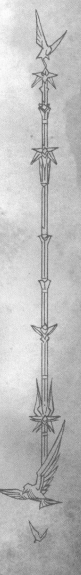

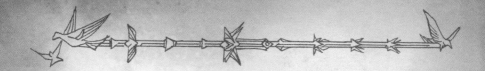

Not all of these events have come to pass. I fear that hidden within these cryptic lines are clues to what lies in store for us. In order to better prepare you against this ominous future, the tome you now hold in your hands compiles knowledge that will aid in protecting you from a range of dark threats. I elaborate on these subjects—from the betrayer Adria to the Black Soulstone and many more—in the chapters ahead. A great deal of the information contained herein was taken from Cain's writings and Leah's investigation into the End of Days—knowledge that remains vitally important to our cause.

I do not claim these pages contain everything you will need to know in the battles to come. This book is merely a continuation of the research begun by the first Horadrim, carried on by Deckard Cain and, most recently, Leah.

Now, as mankind looks toward its future, this legacy falls to you.

Know that more than ever before, the mortal world is in need of heroes. A time may soon come when you will be asked to make the ultimate sacrifice. If it does, find courage in the memory of Uldyssian, Tal Rasha, Deckard Cain, and Leah. Remember all they overcame, how they seized the brilliant potential that burns in every human heart.

Above all, remember that no matter how much the future may spiral out of control, how dark the days may become, a single mortal has the power to change not only this world, but the realms beyond.

—Tyrael

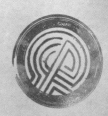

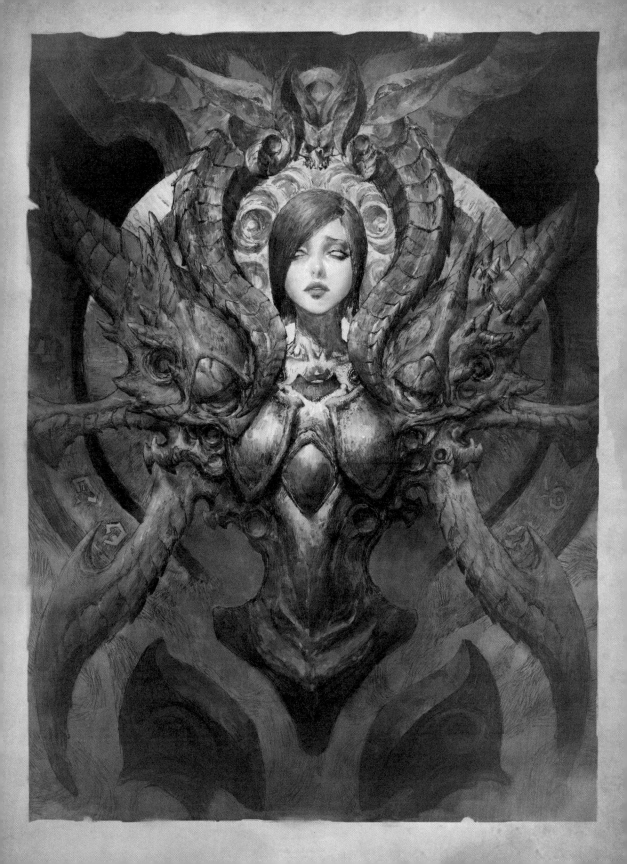

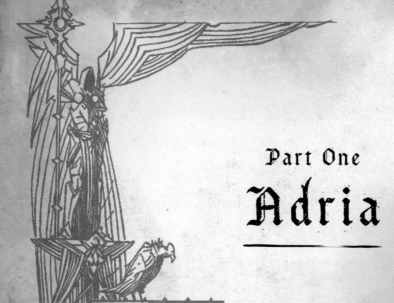

Part One
Adria

T he following is a collection of notes I discovered among Leah's possessions in Bastion's Keep. It includes an investigation of her mother's past written by Cain and accompanied by personal journal entries and notes from Leah. I do not know Adria's current whereabouts, but I believe she is still alive. Read the following passages carefully, for they may contain critical information to use against the betrayer should you cross paths with her again.

As I look back on recent events, it's hard to believe how much
has happened. For one, I finally reunited with my mother, Adria.
Together we recovered the Black Soulstone, a relic created by the
renegade Horadrim Zoltun Kulle. Then, just days ago, Belial nearly
destroyed Caldeum. I can still picture the meteors raining from the
sky, shattering the city's great spires and snuffing out so many
innocent lives.

But the thing I remember most is losing Uncle Deckard. I'm
haunted by that day in New Tristram, the feeling of helplessness
as I watched him take his last breath.

Being in Caldeum only makes the memory of it more painful.
My uncle loved this city. Everywhere I look, I'm reminded of the time
we spent here throughout the years, exploring the narrow alleyways,
sifting through piles of dusty scrolls in the Great Library. Now, the
only real connection I have with him is the research he left me.

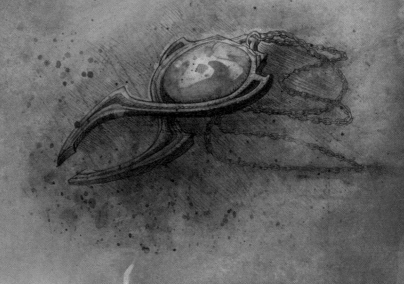

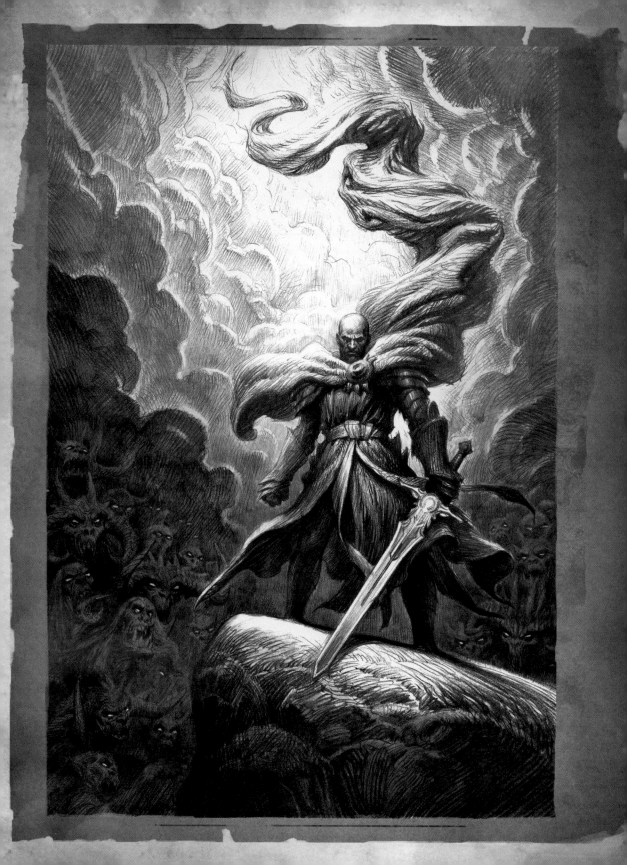

The End of Days. I can't remember how many times Uncle Deckard went on about the Prophecy, muttering the words under his breath. How did he carry on this tedious work for so long? There's no end to the books. It would take a lifetime to get through them all. Just this morning, I found a new journal among his things. I know I should open it, but I'm afraid that if I do, I will only be left with more questions.

I feel as if Tyrael, Adria, and the nephalem are expecting me to make some kind of breakthrough. They believe I have all the answers, but the truth is that I don't know a damned thing. They are the ones with the real power.

I wish Uncle Deckard were here to guide me. I wish I could tell him everything that's happened. Tyrael has regained his memories, and whenever he tells me about the Angiris Council or the High Heavens, all I can think of is how much Uncle would have loved to hear the stories.

Most of all, I just want to hear his voice one last time. I want him to tell me that he's alright. He always said there was something waiting for us after death. A paradise.

I hope you found it, Uncle. I hope it's everything you dreamed it would be.

—Leah

The Witch of Tristram

Is it so strange? He described Mother to me so many times, I could picture her in my head.

Leah has been asking about her mother with growing frequency. I expected this would happen when we set out for New Tristram. Even so, it vexes me. This town has a way of dredging up dark memories, most of which are better left forgotten.

On the first day we arrived, Leah sketched a portrait of Adria that filled me with disquiet. Despite having never really met her mother, she created a perfect likeness of the woman. Perhaps being so close to the teetering remains of Adria's hut has awakened something in Leah. I have warned her not to linger around that place, but she does not listen.

Can I blame her for wanting to know more about her mother? Truth be told, I find my thoughts drifting more and more to Adria as well. For some time now I have toyed with the idea of sifting through the mountain of notes I have written about her. At long last, I feel I have enough information to paint an accurate picture. And I suppose there is no better place to do so than here in Tristram, where I met the witch.

So then, what do I know of Adria? She is an enigma I fear I will never understand. At times she has appeared suspect, while at others noble and even caring. What I can say with certainty, however, is that she is a driven and fiercely intelligent person, bristling with a mix of grace, beauty, and raw, frightening power.

I first encountered her during the Darkening of Tristram. She arrived in the town as many others were fleeing. As such, I regarded her with suspicion. Seemingly overnight, she constructed a small hut at the town's edge, where she sold strange arcane artifacts and tomes of knowledge, a great deal of which even I had never seen before.

Eventually I worked up the courage to speak with her. To my delight, I discovered she was well-versed in ancient history. We would often spend hours in the Tavern of the Rising Sun, discussing the great battles of the Mage Clan Wars, the mysteries surrounding the Zakarum

This doesn't seem to be addressed to anyone in particular. Is it one of Uncle's personal journals?

faith's origins, and the Sin War. In particular, she possessed an interest in the Horadrim and tales related to Zoltun Kulle and the Black Soulstone.

Discussed in the Book of Cain.

Her curiosity never alarmed me. Quite the contrary, I quickly grew to admire Adria. The two of us believed that knowledge was the most powerful weapon at our disposal. We supplied information to Prince Aidan and his companions, helping them in their battle against the demonic forces that threatened Tristram.

But always I sensed that the witch was searching for some lost truth among those old stories. Unfortunately, I never had a chance to find out what that was. After the Lord of Terror's defeat, Adria vanished from Tristram just as suddenly as she had arrived.

The witch had no reason to stay; Diablo's reign of terror was at an end. Even so, her departure filled me with a deep and overwhelming sense of loss. There was something almost contagious about Adria's ambition and confidence. In a way, it was through her that I began living up to my Horadric lineage, albeit far too late to spare the people of Tristram from the horrors they faced.

I later learned that Adria had taken the barmaid Gillian east to Caldeum, where the witch had then given birth to Leah. Adria, however, had not stayed to care for her child. She had left the city on some mysterious errand, leaving poor Gillian to raise the infant.

As the years passed, I heard rumor that Adria had perished in the Dreadlands, but I knew nothing of the circumstances surrounding her death, nor did I have the inclination to pursue the truth. My investigation into the End of Days consumed my every waking hour. Adria and our time together became a distant memory.

But fate is a bewildering force, always leading us on inexplicable paths. My life became intertwined with Adria's once again when I visited Leah and Gillian in Caldeum. Madness had

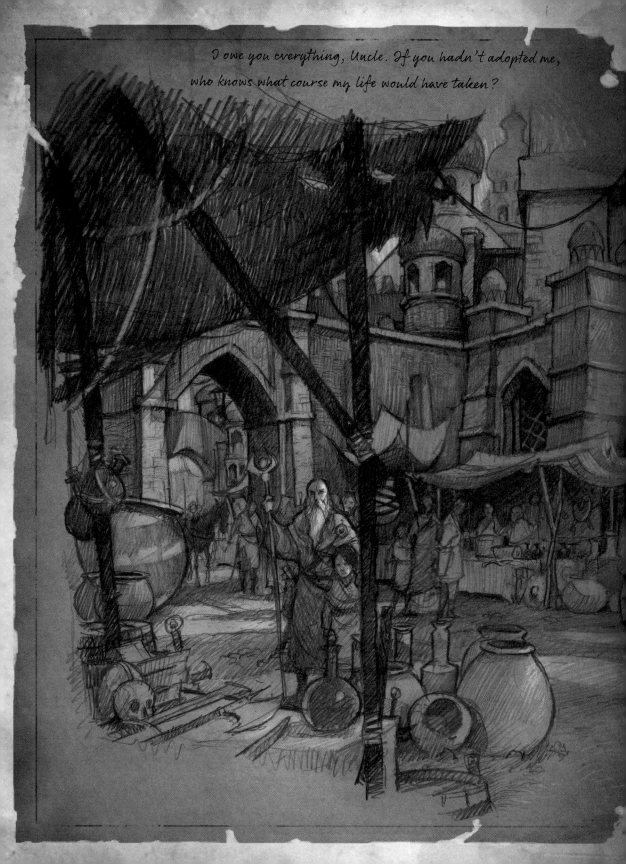

I owe you everything, Uncle. If you hadn't adopted me, who knows what course my life would have taken?

sapped the barmaid of her youth and optimism (as it had with many of those who were in the path of the Prime Evils). Not fit to watch over Leah any longer, she was committed to a madhouse in the northern part of the city, and I was left to care for Adria's daughter.

Oh, how my life changed that day. Admittedly, I was wary of the child. She displayed a disturbing affinity to magic even more potent than Adria's. The young girl often awoke in the dead of night, terrified by strange nightmares. Sometimes, it seemed that she would move and act without conscious thought. But I knew that beneath it all she possessed a pure heart, filled with courage and hope.

Leah became my protégé. I dragged her to so many strange and faraway places, hunting clues to the End of Days wherever I could find them. Quite unexpectedly, her presence gave my quest even greater meaning. I redoubled my efforts, knowing there was nothing more important to fight for than Leah and the future she represented.

On a more personal level, she reawakened something within me that I had thought lost forever: the joy and love of having a family. Leah began more and more to remind me of my own child, the son who had died so many years ago. She forced me to face and overcome the mistakes of my past . . . the things I had tried to hide from for far too long. Although I did not deserve it, Leah gave me a second chance at life. She made me a better person. For that, I can never repay her.

But I digress. Leah's presence also rekindled my interest in Adria. It seemed more important than ever to learn about the witch now that I was caring for her daughter. I resolved to look into her past when I had the time to spare. I promised myself that whatever information I learned, I would pass it on to Leah.

All these years later, I have failed to keep that promise.

My investigation of Adria quickly became an obsession, vying in importance with my End of Days research. Even so, I kept all of my discoveries a secret from Leah.

Often I wonder if it was right to do so. Doesn't she, above all others, deserve to know?

Perhaps, but something akin to instinct has kept me from telling her more. As a scholar, I look to facts for guidance. I have never been one to put much faith in my "gut." In this case, however, that is all I have to rely on. I only hope I have made the right choice.

27th day of Ratham

1285 Anno Kehjistani

I can't sleep.

We're setting off for Bastion's Keep tomorrow morning. Azmodan is rallying his legions to besiege the ancient fortress, and I'm anxious about what we'll find when we get there.

But there's another reason I'm still awake. I can't stop thinking about Uncle Deckard's journal. Why didn't he tell me he knew so much about my mother? He always used to say she was dead. Was he lying all that time? Did he think I'd be frightened by the truth?

I guess there's no point getting angry about it now. Knowing Uncle, he probably thought he was protecting me by keeping the truth guarded. His choice, as much as I disagree with it, was born of good intentions.

None of that changes the fact that I'm stuck with this journal, though. In some small way, I feel like I'm betraying Uncle Deckard by continuing to read it. Then again, if he left it among his things, he must've suspected that I would find it one day.

Why am I going on about this? It's strange that with battle looming ahead — with the fate of everything hanging in the balance — I'm letting a single journal bother me.

It's probably best if I just put it aside, maybe leave it here in Caldeum until all this madness is over. The last thing I need right now is something else to worry over.

I'll decide in the morning. It's growing late, and I need to rest.

—Leah

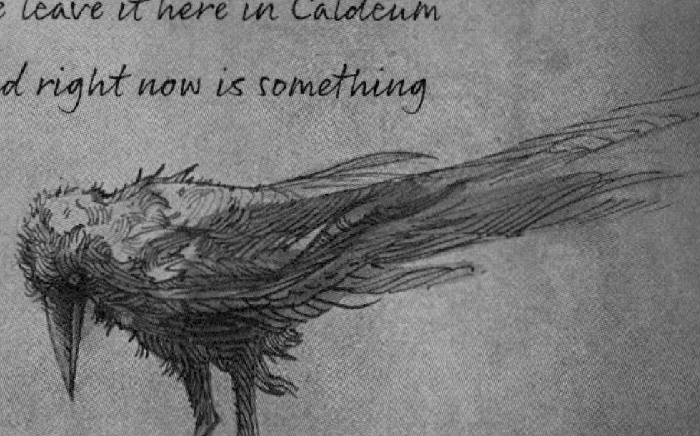

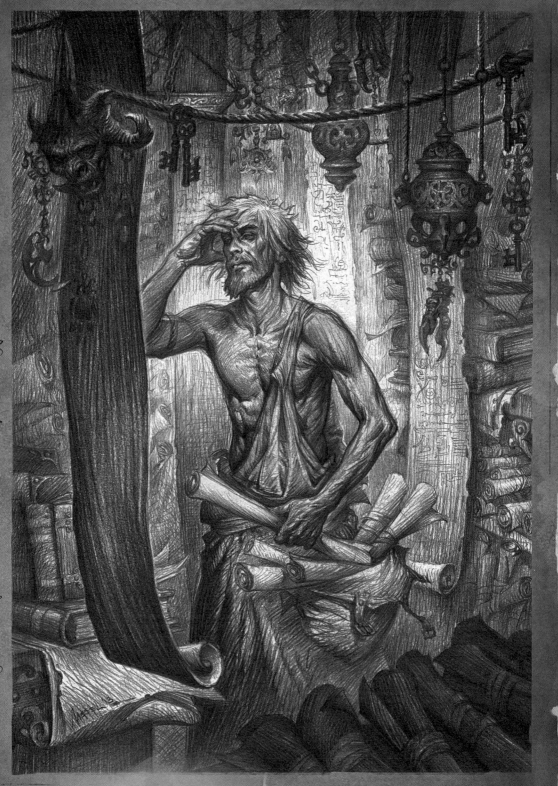

Throughout his life, Uncle Deckard was always searching for answers.

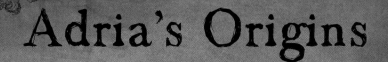

Adria's Origins

To truly understand someone, you must know the circumstances of their upbringing. And so it was that when I began investigating Adria, I looked first to her childhood.

One night in Tristram, I asked Adria about her origins, but she said only that her father had been a merchant. Aside from that, she deflected or ignored my subsequent questions about her past. I did, however, glean other clues from the time I spent with her. Most of the spells and apothecary recipes she knew were commonly used by the reclusive witches who dwelled in Westmarch. Her voice also had faint traces of an accent (one, it seems, she was trying to hide) that marked her as being born and raised along the docks of Kingsport. The style of speech in that part of the coastal city is unmistakable, even compared to the other population centers of Westmarch.

Thus, during a trip to Westmarch in search of an ancient Zakarum cipher, I visited the docking quarter of Kingsport. Quite by luck, I met one of the city's retired constables, a man nearly as old as I am now. Having lived and worked in the area his entire life, he immediately recognized the name Adria.

Her father, Sevrin, hailed from a long line of powerful merchants. He was an unstable sort of fellow, the kind prone to sudden acts of wanton violence. Before Adria's

Never noticed this in her voice.

When I ask Adria about her past, she always changes the subject. Why? What is she hiding?

tenth year, Sevrin lost a small fortune when some of his trade ships were destroyed in a storm. In the fit of rage that followed, he reportedly strangled his wife to death. The constable and city guards arrested the man and charged him with murder, a crime punishable by hanging. But due to his wealth and influence, Sevrin secured a pardon and was thereafter released from prison.

What I find strange is that Adria did not run off during this series of events. On the contrary, the constable said the young girl lingered outside the jailhouse. When Sevrin was released, the two of them went back to living at their dockside abode.

Buying his way out of prison had leeched away Sevrin's wealth. Gradually, he fell into heavy debt and made a number of dangerous enemies. The constable claimed that not long after these events, Sevrin's home caught fire in the dead of night. City guards rushed to douse the flames. According to one of the official reports:

> Akarat's bane, the fire burned with unnatural wrath. Two guards succumbed to the inferno, the Light-forsaken heat roasting them in their armor. Water had no noticeable effect on the flames at first. It took a full day to extinguish the blaze.

When the ashes settled, only charred bone remained of Sevrin. As for Adria, one of the first guards to arrive reported seeing a young girl standing outside staring intently at the flames before vanishing into the shadows. While it seems logical that one of Sevrin's rival merchants would have set this killing in motion, I cannot help but think Adria played some part.

I know only bits and pieces concerning Adria's whereabouts and activities following this tragic event. It appears she fled to the wilderness around Kingsport, and perhaps even traveled as far north as the kingdom's capital (also named Westmarch). The fact that she did so at such a young age is testament to her resourcefulness and willpower.

What I know with certainty is that she eventually became involved with a small and secretive group of witches that existed in the region's remote wilds.

It's difficult to believe she would have stayed so loyal to her father, only to kill him later.

I remember this trip. Uncle never told me what we were doing there. He had me stay with an old friend of his while he went to look for the Zakarum cipher.

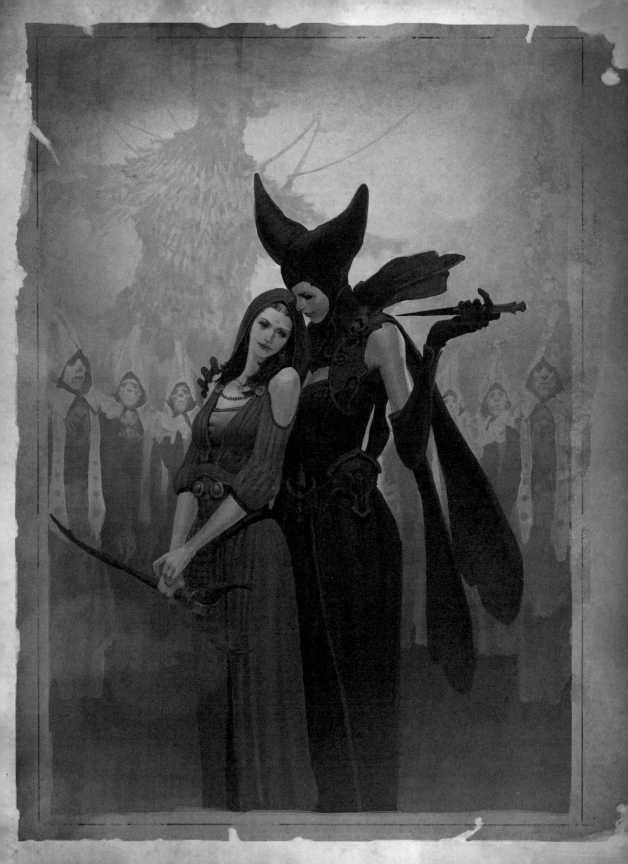

Over the years, she became a powerful figure within this circle.

My first real clue as to Adria's more recent activities came while investigating the Coven for its potential ties to the End of Days. I consider this group to be a remnant of the Triune, the ancient religion created by Diablo, Baal, and Mephisto to turn the hearts of mankind to darkness. The violent events of the Sin War had shattered the Triune, splitting it into vestigial groups with no coherent leadership.

In the centuries that followed, it languished in ignominy, scorned and ostracized by greater society. The Triune experienced a slight resurgence in the time we know of as the Dark Exile, but it quickly faded when the Horadrim imprisoned the Prime Evils.

It was not until my own lifetime that the cult rose to power again in the western lands, under the name of the Coven. By all accounts, it appears that two witches joined the floundering cult and poisoned its leaders. These usurpers then took control of the Coven, reforging it into a dangerous new order that practiced torture and demonic summoning. It is said these witches were fueled by the belief that they were destined to become mortal heralds of the Burning Hells.

I knew with certainty that one of the leaders was Maghda, a malicious and fanatical individual unopposed to sacrificing her followers in order to achieve her goals. Tales of her cruelty and depravity were what had compelled me

I think at some point the remnants of the Triune shifted from Kehjistan to the west as a way to begin anew. Under Maghda, they crawled back to the east and laid claim to the deserts around Caldeum.

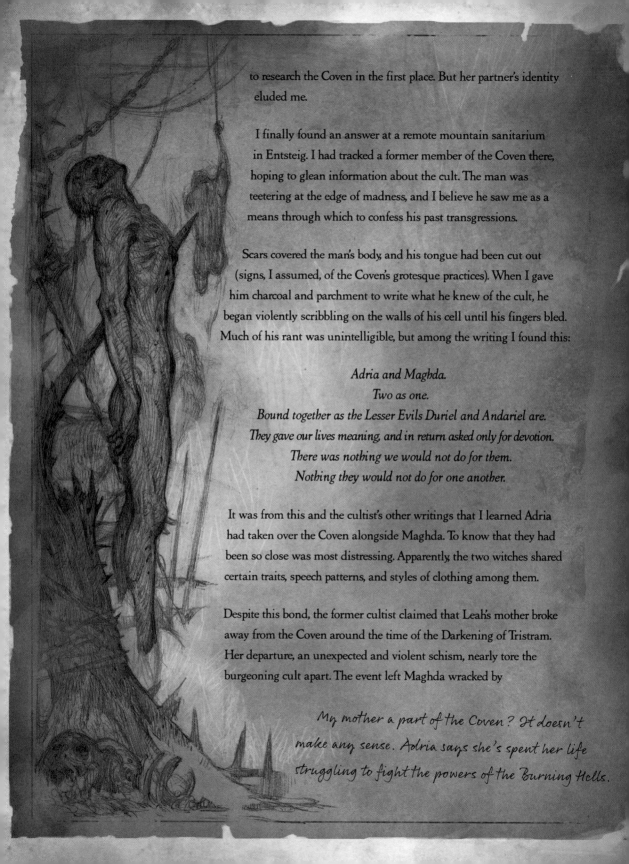

to research the Coven in the first place. But her partner's identity eluded me.

I finally found an answer at a remote mountain sanitarium in Entsteig. I had tracked a former member of the Coven there, hoping to glean information about the cult. The man was teetering at the edge of madness, and I believe he saw me as a means through which to confess his past transgressions.

Scars covered the man's body, and his tongue had been cut out (signs, I assumed, of the Coven's grotesque practices). When I gave him charcoal and parchment to write what he knew of the cult, he began violently scribbling on the walls of his cell until his fingers bled. Much of his rant was unintelligible, but among the writing I found this:

Adria and Maghda.
Two as one.
Bound together as the Lesser Evils Duriel and Andariel are.
They gave our lives meaning, and in return asked only for devotion.
There was nothing we would not do for them.
Nothing they would not do for one another.

It was from this and the cultist's other writings that I learned Adria had taken over the Coven alongside Maghda. To know that they had been so close was most distressing. Apparently, the two witches shared certain traits, speech patterns, and styles of clothing among them.

Despite this bond, the former cultist claimed that Leah's mother broke away from the Coven around the time of the Darkening of Tristram. Her departure, an unexpected and violent schism, nearly tore the burgeoning cult apart. The event left Maghda wracked by

My mother a part of the Coven? It doesn't make any sense. Adria says she's spent her life struggling to fight the powers of the Burning Hells.

jealousy and rage. Fueled by these dark
emotions, she redoubled her efforts to contact
the Burning Hells. I have suspicions that Belial,
the Lord of Lies, or Azmodan, the Lord of Sin,
answered her call, although clear evidence to
support this theory remains elusive.

As for Adria, she had washed away all signs of
her association with the Coven by the time she came to
Tristram. Looking back, I wonder if she had reinvented
her identity. Or, had she merely reverted back to her true
self? Was the person I met and spent so many hours
talking with the real Adria? Or was that just another
mask she wore?

Of greater concern was why Adria left the cult in the
first place. I want to believe she saw the error of her ways,
but the truth is not so simple. Maghda had always been
devoted to the cult, but Adria seemed only to be passing
through, driven by the allure of power. If there is one thing
I know about her, it is that she acts with purpose.

With all of this in mind, I suspect that Adria sought me out
in Tristram to learn what she could of the Horadrim and
other old lore in my possession. But were her intentions for
good or for ill? What new goal did she see shimmering on
the horizon?

It would be a number of years before I finally discovered
an answer to these questions.

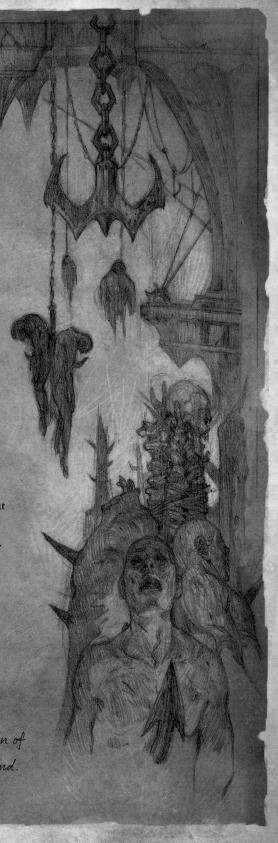

*I haven't told Adria about the journal yet.
I need more time to think over what I've read.
    The last thing I want to do is ruin her opinion of
Uncle Deckard. She always considered him a friend.*

3rd day of Kathon

1285 Anno Kehjistani

My whole life, I've suffered from terrible nightmares. Dreams of blood
and war, of bloated corpses pecked down to the bones by giant crows.
Their oil-black eyes glaring at me with hate, filling me with foreboding.
Other times, I dream of angels and demons with frightening clarity, as
if the things I'm seeing are more akin to memories than figments of my
imagination.

   Ever since we recovered the Black Soulstone, the nightmares have only
gotten worse. Keeping vigil over the crystal takes up nearly all of my time.
I can sense the five Evils trapped within it, watching me. They batter against
the prison's walls, screaming in my head.

   My mother's lessons are the only things that help me stay in control.
Each day, she teaches me how to harness my magic and use it to contain the
darkness inside the soulstone. She's strict and demanding, but fair. She never
gives up on me.

   At first, I was hesitant to take Adria's advice. Uncle Deckard tried,
unsuccessfully, to help me control my gift, but the training never really
changed anything. He said my abilities were dangerous. Through Adria's
lessons, I've begun seeing things differently. This power—it's a natural
part of me. Using it makes me feel like I've tapped into something
that's always yearned to be set free. For the first time since
leaving New Tristram, I have the sense that
I can make a real difference in our
battle against the forces of the Hells.

      —Leah

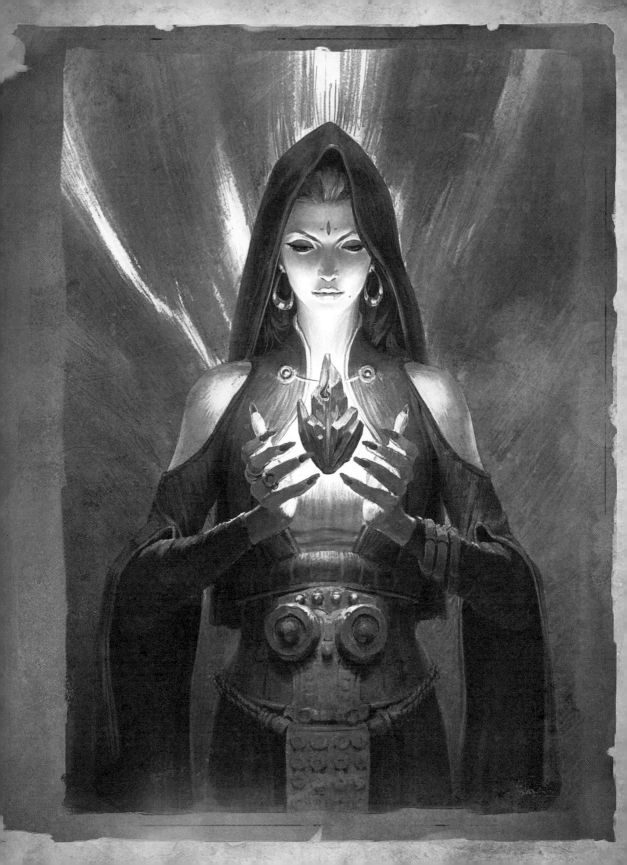

Adria's Quest

In the years following my trip to the Entsteig sanitarium, I would often sense Adria's presence nearby. Leah would unexpectedly ask about her mother at these times, or feverishly repeat the witch's name in the throes of a restless sleep. But Adria remained hidden, eluding my attempts to track her down.

What purpose brought the witch so near to us? Was she checking on the well-being of her daughter, or had we crossed paths with Adria merely by chance?

These vexing questions gnawed at me, leading to many sleepless nights. Before long it became quite difficult to maintain focus on my pressing End of Days investigation. To my relief, I at long last found answers while conducting research in Caldeum's Great Library. A fellow scholar told me of a witch matching Adria's description who had recently passed through the city. He claimed she had visited the library, inquiring about famous battles fought during the Sin War and Mage Clan Wars. The Desolate Sands, the gates of ancient Viz-jun, and the ruins of the Cathedral of Light—these were the names relayed to me.

Immediately, I realized the significance of the scholar's tale. In Tristram, Adria and I had discussed these same historical sites. They were places that the notorious Horadrim Zoltun Kulle had frequented centuries ago. According to some mages and scholars, angels and demons had perished at many of these locations.

And with that revelation, the shards of half-truths began taking greater shape. Adria had always been strangely fascinated with Kulle and, in particular, his most deplorable creation: the Black Soulstone. Had this been her quest all these years? To seek the cursed artifact out?

Mother admitted her connection to the Coven. She says it was part of her quest to wage war against the Hells, but she confesses she went too far. I haven't told Tyrael or the others. I can't. They might lose trust in Adria at a time when we need to work together most.

Sometimes a longing to see her would overcome me. It lasted for hours. Days, even.

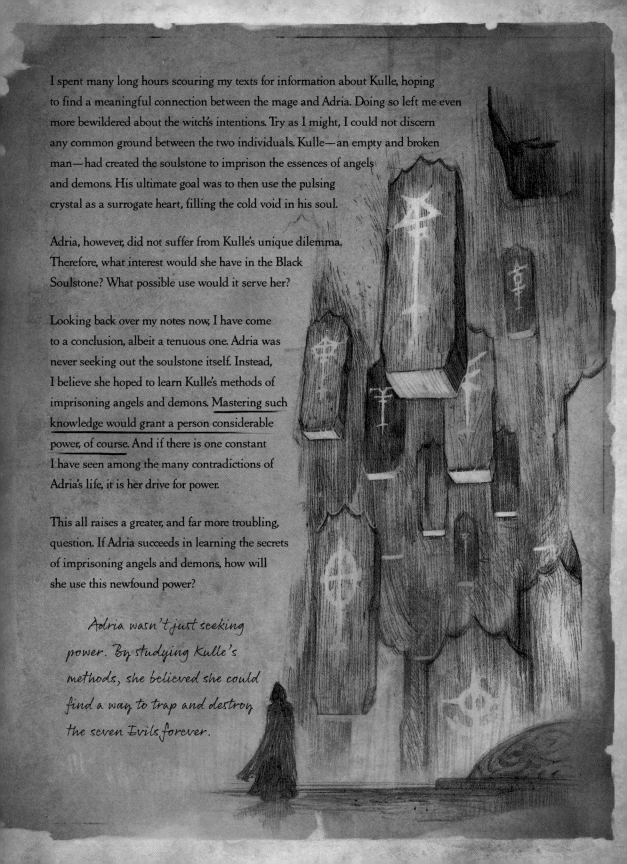

I spent many long hours scouring my texts for information about Kulle, hoping to find a meaningful connection between the mage and Adria. Doing so left me even more bewildered about the witch's intentions. Try as I might, I could not discern any common ground between the two individuals. Kulle—an empty and broken man—had created the soulstone to imprison the essences of angels and demons. His ultimate goal was to then use the pulsing crystal as a surrogate heart, filling the cold void in his soul.

Adria, however, did not suffer from Kulle's unique dilemma. Therefore, what interest would she have in the Black Soulstone? What possible use would it serve her?

Looking back over my notes now, I have come to a conclusion, albeit a tenuous one. Adria was never seeking out the soulstone itself. Instead, I believe she hoped to learn Kulle's methods of imprisoning angels and demons. Mastering such knowledge would grant a person considerable power, of course. And if there is one constant I have seen among the many contradictions of Adria's life, it is her drive for power.

This all raises a greater, and far more troubling, question. If Adria succeeds in learning the secrets of imprisoning angels and demons, how will she use this newfound power?

Adria wasn't just seeking power. By studying Kulle's methods, she believed she could find a way to trap and destroy the seven Evils forever.

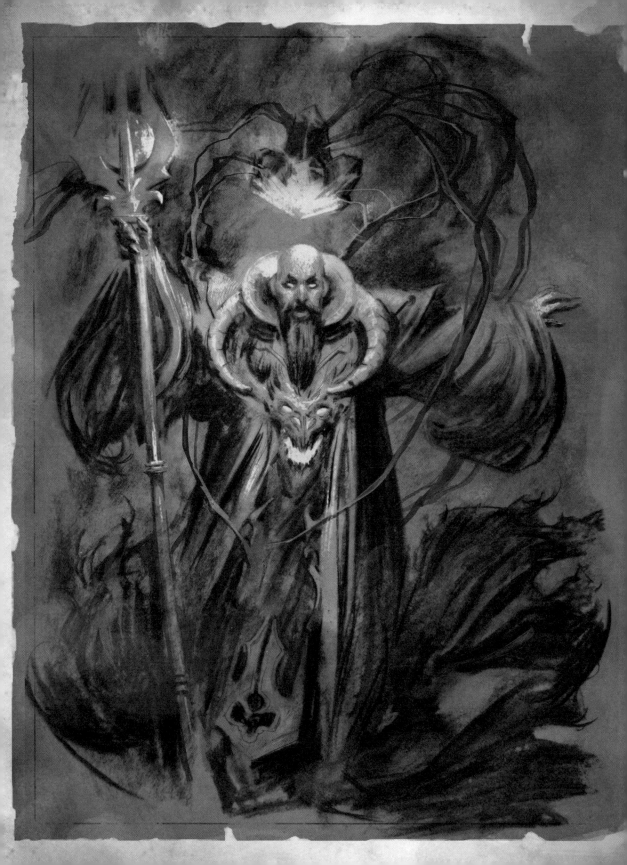

Zoltun Kulle and the Black Soulstone

I have spent many years documenting historical figures. In all that time, very few have filled me with equal parts disgust and reverence. Zoltun Kulle is one of them.

Ancient texts portray him in a number of different ways: a once virtuous man lost to the dark abyss of obsession, a murderer and a torturer, and a heroic member of the Horadrim. But most of all, he is known as the architect of the Black Soulstone, a profane simulacrum of the three crystals Archangel Tyrael bestowed on the Horadrim.

Over the following pages, I will examine how he accomplished such a feat and also speculate on what his ultimate intentions were.

To begin, it is very important to understand Kulle's origins. He hailed from the Ennead mage clan, a group renowned for its mastery of transmutation and enchantment. Like his kin, Kulle dedicated his life to the noble pursuit of these sciences, always seeking to manipulate the base components of the physical world.

Jered Cain, in *The Nature of the Soulstones*, succinctly described Kulle this way:

> In all things, he glimpsed the elements of life, ripe for growth. He was, in his better
> days, driven by dreams of elevating his fellow man to wondrous new heights.
> Kulle, perhaps above all other Horadrim, had the power and the wisdom to bring
> his grand vision of a better world—one devoid of its inherent flaws—to fruition.

During the Hunt for the Three, Tal Rasha entrusted Kulle with the vital task of safeguarding the Amber, Sapphire, and Crimson Soulstones. The Ennead mage's expertise in the realm of physical objects made him the perfect choice for such an undertaking. Jered wrote that he often found Kulle awake late into the night, experimenting with the soulstones and documenting their properties.

Uncle Deckard referenced multiple texts about Zoltun Kulle, but I could only find this among his things.

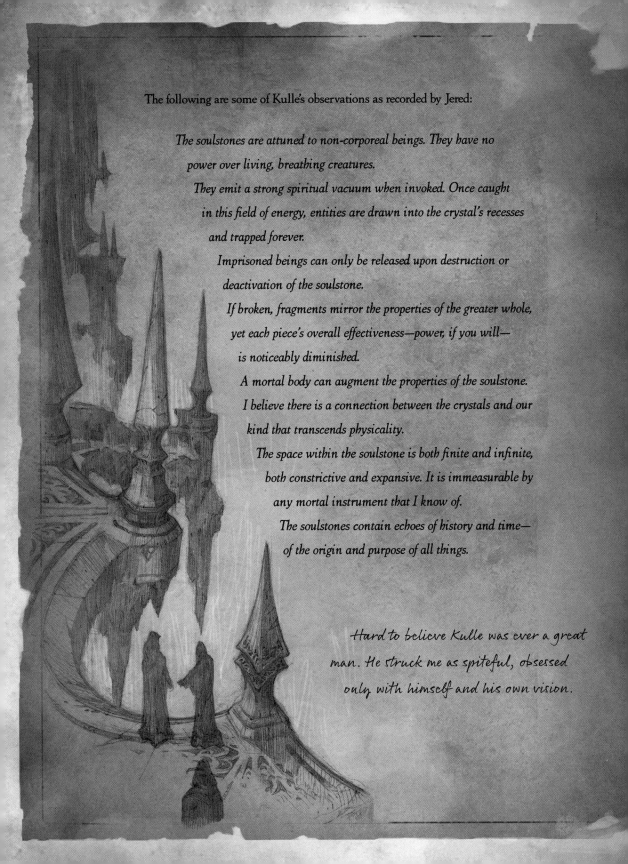

The following are some of Kulle's observations as recorded by Jered:

The soulstones are attuned to non-corporeal beings. They have no
power over living, breathing creatures.

They emit a strong spiritual vacuum when invoked. Once caught
in this field of energy, entities are drawn into the crystal's recesses
and trapped forever.

Imprisoned beings can only be released upon destruction or
deactivation of the soulstone.

If broken, fragments mirror the properties of the greater whole,
yet each piece's overall effectiveness—power, if you will—
is noticeably diminished.

A mortal body can augment the properties of the soulstone.

I believe there is a connection between the crystals and our
kind that transcends physicality.

The space within the soulstone is both finite and infinite,
both constrictive and expansive. It is immeasurable by
any mortal instrument that I know of.

The soulstones contain echoes of history and time—
of the origin and purpose of all things.

Hard to believe Kulle was ever a great
man. He struck me as spiteful, obsessed
only with himself and his own vision.

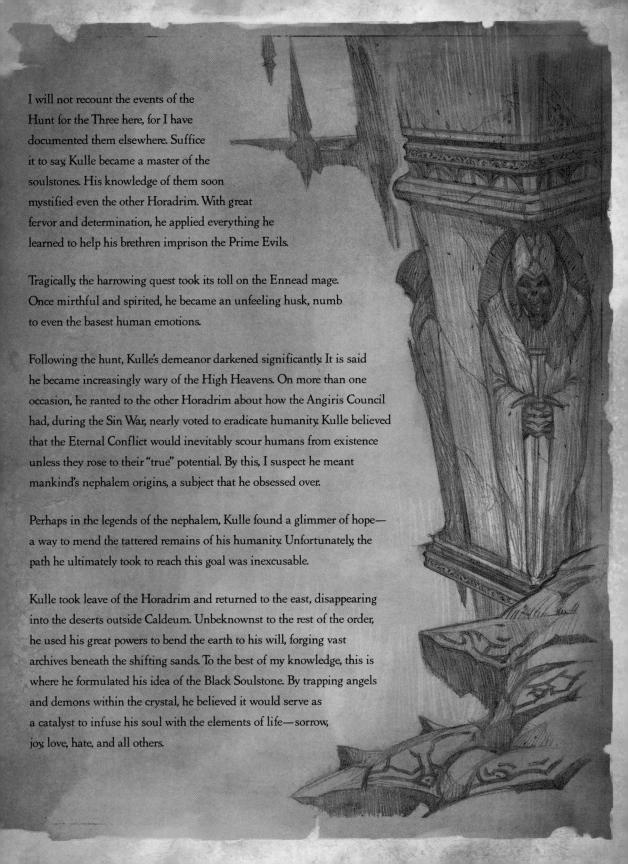

I will not recount the events of the
Hunt for the Three here, for I have
documented them elsewhere. Suffice
it to say, Kulle became a master of the
soulstones. His knowledge of them soon
mystified even the other Horadrim. With great
fervor and determination, he applied everything he
learned to help his brethren imprison the Prime Evils.

Tragically, the harrowing quest took its toll on the Ennead mage.
Once mirthful and spirited, he became an unfeeling husk, numb
to even the basest human emotions.

Following the hunt, Kulle's demeanor darkened significantly. It is said
he became increasingly wary of the High Heavens. On more than one
occasion, he ranted to the other Horadrim about how the Angiris Council
had, during the Sin War, nearly voted to eradicate humanity. Kulle believed
that the Eternal Conflict would inevitably scour humans from existence
unless they rose to their "true" potential. By this, I suspect he meant
mankind's nephalem origins, a subject that he obsessed over.

Perhaps in the legends of the nephalem, Kulle found a glimmer of hope—
a way to mend the tattered remains of his humanity. Unfortunately, the
path he ultimately took to reach this goal was inexcusable.

Kulle took leave of the Horadrim and returned to the east, disappearing
into the deserts outside Caldeum. Unbeknownst to the rest of the order,
he used his great powers to bend the earth to his will, forging vast
archives beneath the shifting sands. To the best of my knowledge, this is
where he formulated his idea of the Black Soulstone. By trapping angels
and demons within the crystal, he believed it would serve as
a catalyst to infuse his soul with the elements of life—sorrow,
joy, love, hate, and all others.

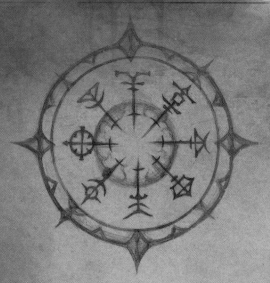

How he actually went about crafting the soulstone remains a great mystery. Not even Jered wrote conclusively on the subject (but perhaps that was intentional). Of the more suspicious reports I have come across, one claims that Kulle drained some of his own blood and transmuted it into crystal. Another account states that the mage excavated the remains of a legendary nephalem and molded the bones into the Black Soulstone.

But these tales are steeped in conjecture and hearsay, and therefore must be viewed with skepticism. The important fact is that Kulle succeeded in creating the soulstone. He then set out to imprison angels and demons within the crystal. For this, the Ennead mage journeyed to sites from the eras of the Sin War and Mage Clan Wars—places where terrible battles had raged between angels, demons, and nephalem.

To fully appreciate Kulle's vision, it is crucial to understand something related to the nature of demons. To the best of my knowledge, when one of these creatures is killed in the mortal realm, it leaves something behind—a shadow of sorts. It might be helpful to think of this shadow as a lingering portion of the demon's essence imprinted on our world.

Angels, however, are an entirely different matter. Very likely, Kulle had developed a different technique for trapping angels than he had for demons, but I am lacking in specifics regarding this.

What I do know, however, is that Kulle used his various techniques to mark angels and the essences of slain demons. He planned to cast a powerful summoning spell that would force them into the recesses of the Black Soulstone.

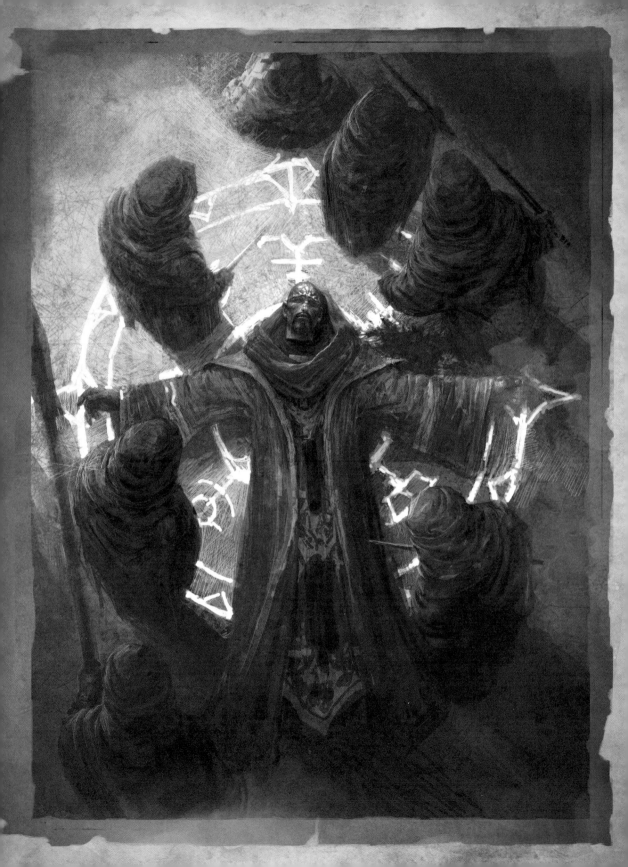

Kulle worked tirelessly to perfect his methods. It is said that he developed an entirely new system of runes for trapping and summoning demons (perhaps influenced in some way by Vizjerei magic). Before long, he had marked a number of sites around Kehjistan.

By this time, the Horadrim had learned of Kulle's intentions. After much deliberation and planning, they stormed the Ennead mage's shadowy archives. Kulle had planned for such a scenario by filling his lair with traps and guardian constructs composed of living sand. One of the Horadrim who took part in the mission—Iben Fahd—wrote that many of these brethren lost their lives during the assault. In the end, however, the Horadrim prevailed. They thwarted Kulle at the precise moment when he was poised to cast his great summoning spell.

Of Kulle's fate, I know that the Horadrim could not kill him—at least not in the normal sense of the word. Perhaps Kulle had truly awakened his nephalem birthright, thereby granting him extraordinary powers. Whatever the case, the Horadrim were forced to undertake a most gruesome task: dismembering Kulle. They concealed his head in the Dahlgur Oasis and locked his body away in what Iben Fahd cryptically referred to as a "Realm of Shadow." I have heard rumors that this place might have been similar to the domains that the ancient Vizjerei used to imprison and interrogate demons.

I am woefully ignorant of what transpired with regards to the Black Soulstone. Did the Horadrim destroy it? Or, as with Kulle, was it beyond their abilities? Knowing the Ennead mage, he would likely have gone to great lengths to protect his masterwork.

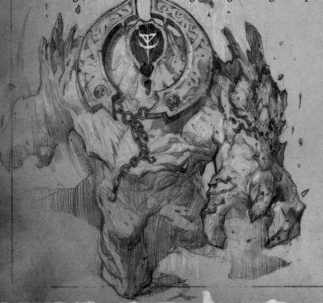

Mother spent years learning how to use Kulle's runes. That's why she couldn't be a part of my life. She negated Kulle's spellwork and then used his magic as a means to somehow mark the Lesser and Prime Evils.

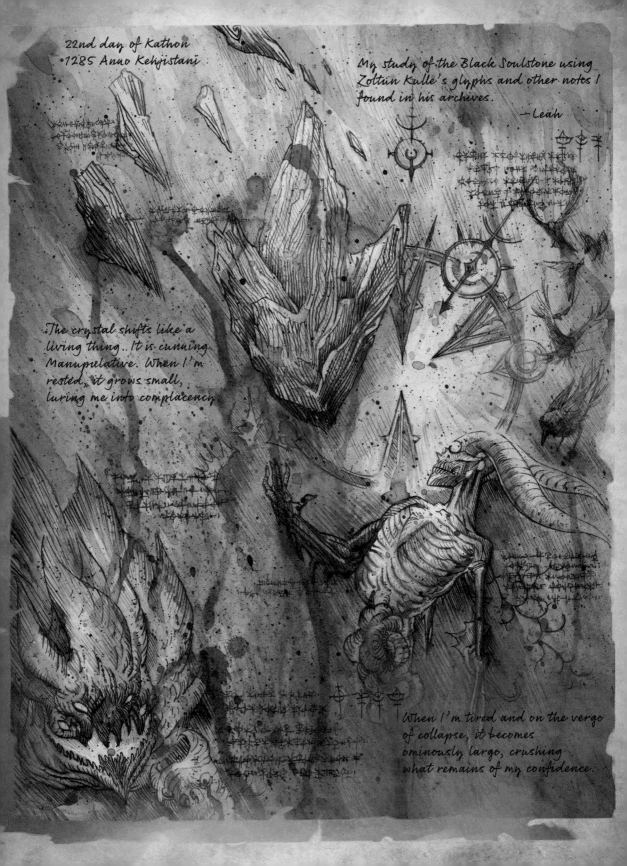

22nd day of Kathon
1285 Anno Kehjistani

My study of the Black Soulstone using
Zoltun Kulle's glyphs and other notes I
found in his archives.

—Leah

The crystal shifts like a
living thing.. It is cunning.
Manipulative. When I'm
rested, it grows small,
luring me into complacency.

When I'm tired and on the verge
of collapse, it becomes
ominously large, crushing
what remains of my confidence.

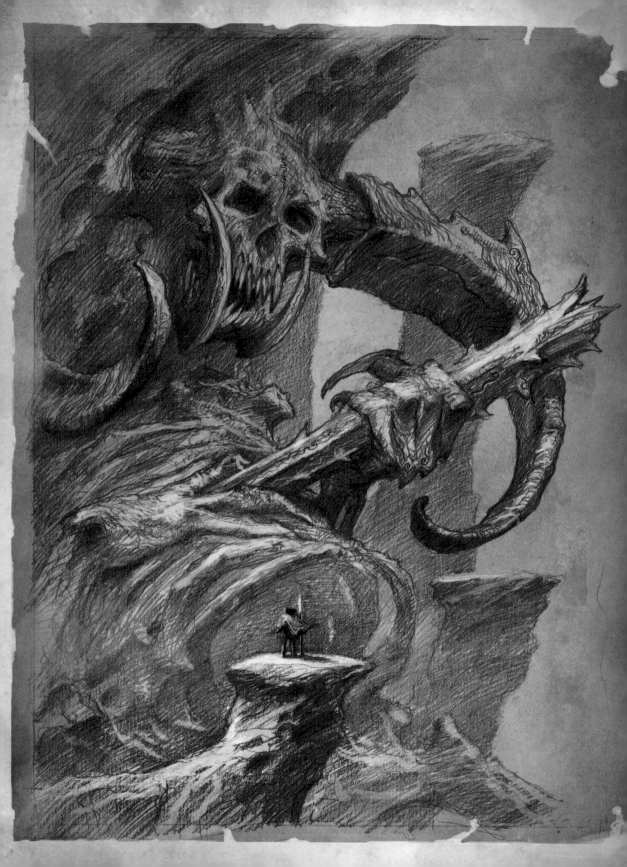

Conclusions

Having reviewed my notes and compiled this manuscript, I must ask again: what do I know of Adria? I am quite loath to admit that answering this question with any certainty seems more untenable now than ever before.

On the one hand, I have uncovered a great deal about Adria's unsavory history. This evidence presents her as a person of shifting allegiances. By all accounts, her life is defined by a perpetual ebb and flow between attachment and abandonment, loyalty and betrayal. For examples of this, I need only look to her dealings with individuals such as Sevrin and Maghda. From all of this, I would conclude that Adria cares only for the people around her so long as they prove useful to her mysterious goals. The drive for knowledge and power dictates every facet of her relationships.

On the other hand, I have met Adria myself, and I have judged her as a courageous and brilliant, albeit unconventional, ally. In Old Tristram, I believed her when she said her grand mission was to wage war against the Evils of the Burning Hells. I would even go so far as to say that, in a very meaningful way, she inspired me to set out on my current path.

But how can I reconcile my own firsthand experiences with the knowledge that she once led the Coven, a cult that exists to serve the very forces she claimed to stand against? Oh, if only I could meet Adria again and put my mind at ease. I have so many questions for her. Perhaps she has an explanation for those unsettling chapters of her past.

Deep down, I want to believe that she has overcome whatever dark thoughts led her to join the Coven and, later, rule it alongside Maghda. I want to believe that this strange quest she embarked on years ago and her obsession with Zoltun Kulle are both in the interest of good rather than evil. I wish this all for my own sake, but even more so for Leah's.

This wish, however, also stems from an altogether different concern. In conducting my End of Days research, thoughts of Adria have continually plagued me. For the life of me, I cannot understand the reason. Why, when I have so vital and demanding a task at hand, do I spend even a moment worrying about her? Is it simply because Leah is now in my life, or does Adria have some yet unforeseen part to play in future events?

The bitter truth is that I do not know, and I fear I never truly will.

She made hard choices to fight evil. Gave everything of herself. Mother walked a different path than you, Uncle. Doesn't mean her way was wrong.

1st day of Ostara

1285 Anno Kehjistani

It seems as if only a few days have passed since I was rifling through Uncle Deckard's books in Caldeum, but I know it's been much longer. Time is bleeding together. Losing its significance. I spend night and day holed up in this corner of Bastion's Keep.

Mother says the nephalem and Tyrael have routed Azmodan's forces. When we first arrived here, the demon lord was throwing everything against the keep — legions crashing against the walls, sending tremors through the bones of the great fortress. It's over now. If things continue going well, we will soon imprison Azmodan in the Black Soulstone along with the other Evils.

But it's so hard to be hopeful. Hard to think about anything other than the soulstone. The Evils — they know the end is coming. They're growing desperate. Frantic. The energy radiating from the crystal is changing how I see things. How I feel things. Sometimes my body seems to stretch apart at a thousand different points until the pain makes me black out. Other times I have the sensation I'm being crushed, my body folding inward over and over again until the darkness swallows me.

Mother tells me to sleep, but it's getting harder to do so. I always dream of New Tristram and Uncle Deckard. He's sitting at his desk, leafing through his books. I hear laughter drifting through the window of his house. I smell bacon sizzling in the tavern nearby. For a brief moment, everything is normal again.

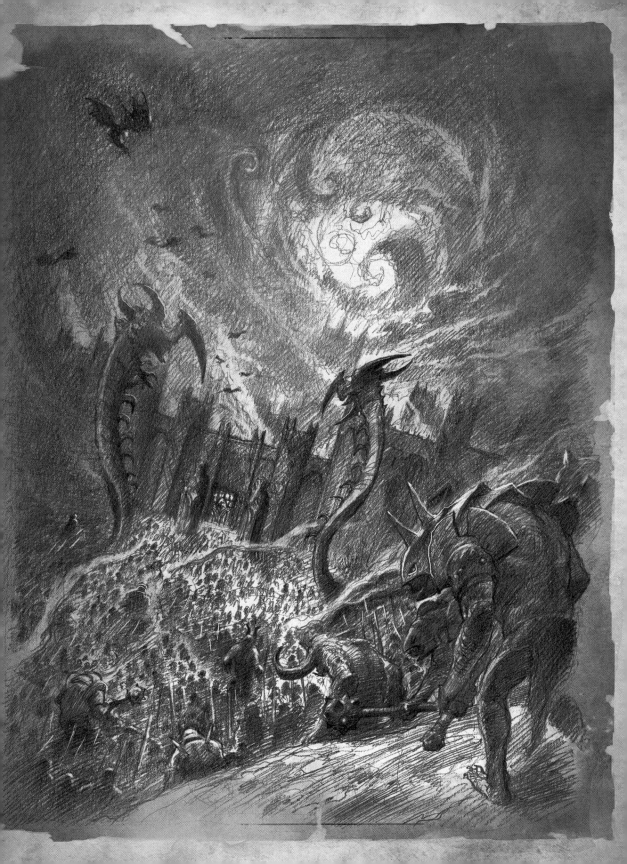

Then I wake up. The laughter becomes the death rattle of injured soldiers in the next room; the smell of bacon becomes the stench of corpses burning on the ramparts.

The realization of everything I've lost presses down on me until I can't move. But Mother knows how to bring me back from the edge. She takes my Horadric necklace and puts it into my hand. The cold metal's touch reminds me to be strong. If I fail, all the dead in New Tristram, Caldeum, and Bastion's Keep will have lost their lives for nothing. All the years Uncle Deckard sacrificed to forestall the End of Days will have been wasted.

I haven't given up, Uncle. We're so close to victory, and we owe so much of it to Mother. I understand why you doubted her. I only wish you could be here to see how hard she's fighting—see how she's the one thing that keeps me going.

Whenever I stumble, she's at my side, holding me. Telling me how proud she is. How much she's missed me these long years. We talk about the things we'll do when the battle is over. She urges me to push forward just a little longer so that everything we've worked for will come to fruition. She promises me that this pain will all be over soon. Then, we will begin our life together anew.

—Leah

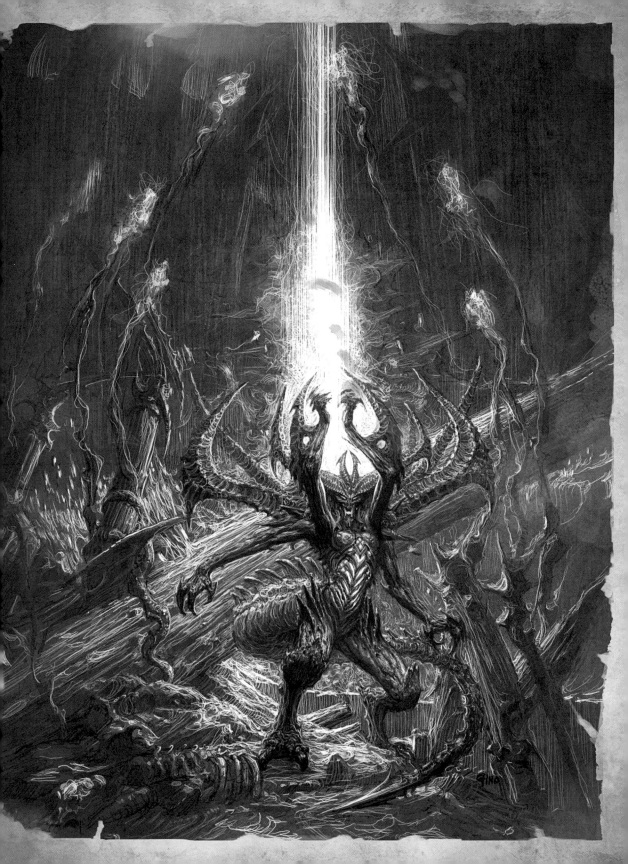

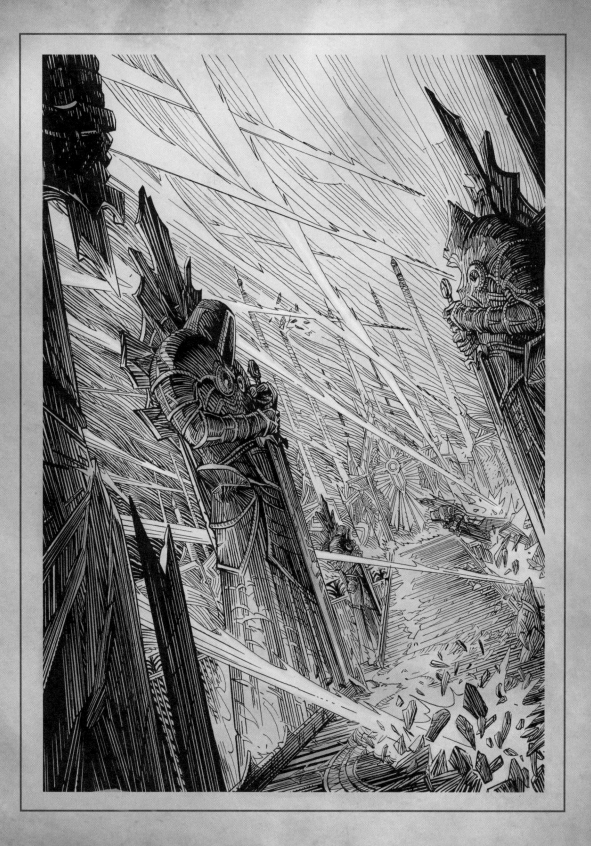

Part Two
The Fate of the Black Soulstone

Being Mortal

I will not say my time acclimating to mortal life has been easy. Of the many facets of this new existence, even something as fundamental as sleep was challenging to accept. Angels have no need of slumber, and I was only vaguely aware of this concept through my past dealings with mankind. During my first days as a mortal, I fought my body's many cries for sleep until exhaustion took me. The strange dreams that followed filled me with disquiet. They were enigmas, storms of images and emotions birthed beyond rational thought.

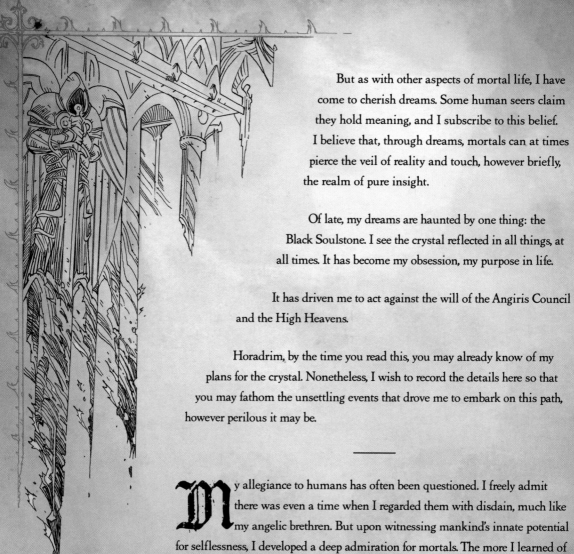

But as with other aspects of mortal life, I have come to cherish dreams. Some human seers claim they hold meaning, and I subscribe to this belief. I believe that, through dreams, mortals can at times pierce the veil of reality and touch, however briefly, the realm of pure insight.

Of late, my dreams are haunted by one thing: the Black Soulstone. I see the crystal reflected in all things, at all times. It has become my obsession, my purpose in life.

It has driven me to act against the will of the Angiris Council and the High Heavens.

Horadrim, by the time you read this, you may already know of my plans for the crystal. Nonetheless, I wish to record the details here so that you may fathom the unsettling events that drove me to embark on this path, however perilous it may be.

———

My allegiance to humans has often been questioned. I freely admit there was even a time when I regarded them with disdain, much like my angelic brethren. But upon witnessing mankind's innate potential for selflessness, I developed a deep admiration for mortals. The more I learned of them, the more I began to see my own kind in a different light. Ultimately, I became aware of a glaring flaw among the angels.

Know this concerning Heaven's denizens: they are immutable in their adherence to order. Laws govern their existence, guiding their every thought and action. Although this affords angels great strength and unity, it also limits their ability to act.

Nowhere was this flaw more evident than in my dealings with the Angiris Council. The archangels—Imperius, Auriel, Itherael, Malthael, and I—were bound by law not to interfere with the mortal realm. But where I only loosely followed this rule, the other council members observed it without question. They obeyed even when the Prime Evils moved to corrupt humanity, threatening to upset the balance of the Eternal Conflict.

When I intervened to forestall catastrophe, the council members chastised me for my recklessness. They ignored my warnings that the Burning Hells would soon assault the mortal world. I came to realize how their precious laws had become more important to them than truth. No amount of arguing or persuading would ever sway them to reason.

I deliberately took on the form of a mortal, sacrificing my angelic essence, in response to the Council's continued inaction. In doing so, I hoped to set an example to the Heavens—to prove that laws can be bent for a greater good.

I also knew that, in time, mankind would hold immeasurable power through its nephalem heritage. Only by standing with humans could I thwart Hell's impending invasion and bridge the gap between the realms of angels and men.

Looking back, I realize how unprepared I was for the realities of mortal existence. As an archangel, I had observed and interacted with humans for centuries. I had watched entire generations come and go, studying the forces that governed their lives. A time even came when I believed that I had learned all there was to know about being mortal.

How wrong I was.

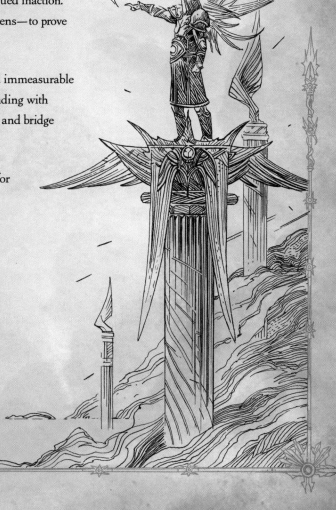

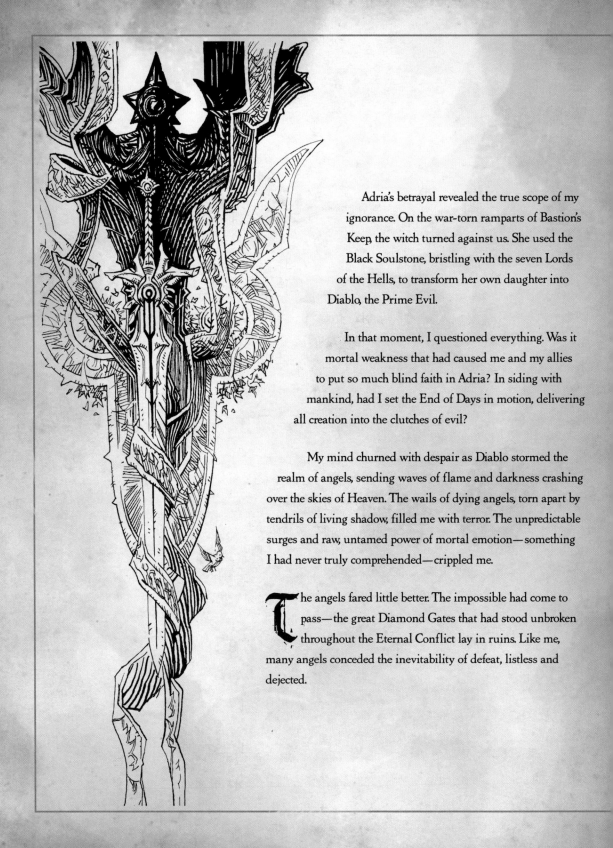

Adria's betrayal revealed the true scope of my ignorance. On the war-torn ramparts of Bastion's Keep, the witch turned against us. She used the Black Soulstone, bristling with the seven Lords of the Hells, to transform her own daughter into Diablo, the Prime Evil.

In that moment, I questioned everything. Was it mortal weakness that had caused me and my allies to put so much blind faith in Adria? In siding with mankind, had I set the End of Days in motion, delivering all creation into the clutches of evil?

My mind churned with despair as Diablo stormed the realm of angels, sending waves of flame and darkness crashing over the skies of Heaven. The wails of dying angels, torn apart by tendrils of living shadow, filled me with terror. The unpredictable surges and raw, untamed power of mortal emotion—something I had never truly comprehended—crippled me.

The angels fared little better. The impossible had come to pass—the great Diamond Gates that had stood unbroken throughout the Eternal Conflict lay in ruins. Like me, many angels conceded the inevitability of defeat, listless and dejected.

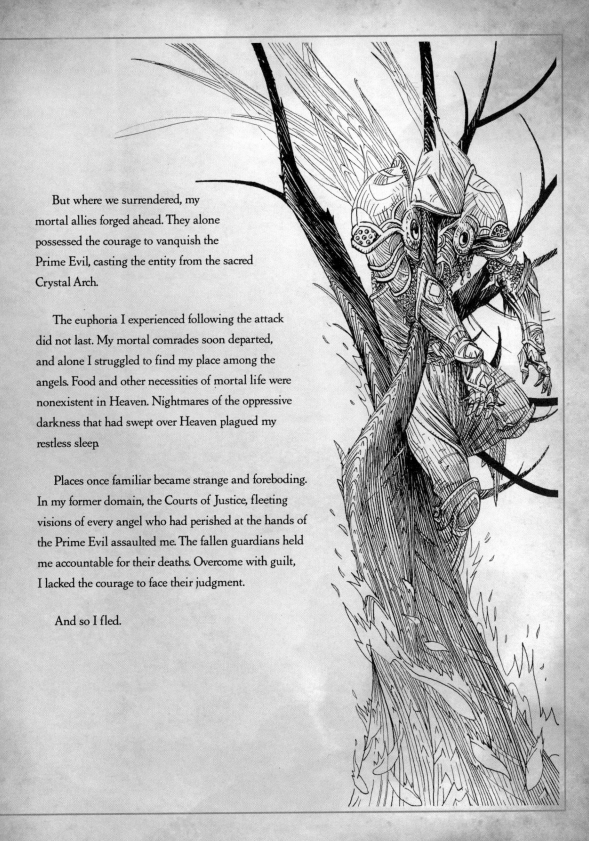

But where we surrendered, my
mortal allies forged ahead. They alone
possessed the courage to vanquish the
Prime Evil, casting the entity from the sacred
Crystal Arch.

The euphoria I experienced following the attack
did not last. My mortal comrades soon departed,
and alone I struggled to find my place among the
angels. Food and other necessities of mortal life were
nonexistent in Heaven. Nightmares of the oppressive
darkness that had swept over Heaven plagued my
restless sleep

Places once familiar became strange and foreboding.
In my former domain, the Courts of Justice, fleeting
visions of every angel who had perished at the hands of
the Prime Evil assaulted me. The fallen guardians held
me accountable for their deaths. Overcome with guilt,
I lacked the courage to face their judgment.

And so I fled.

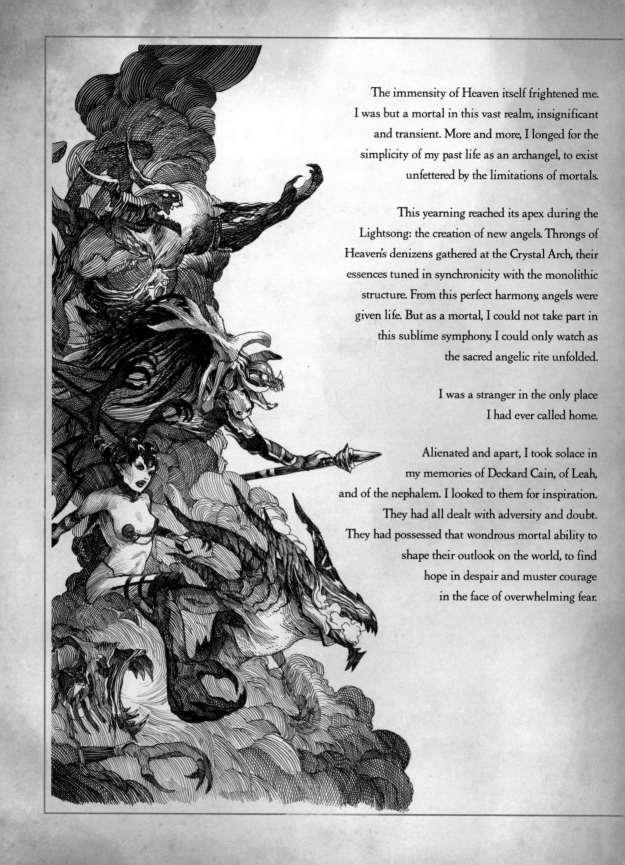

The immensity of Heaven itself frightened me.
I was but a mortal in this vast realm, insignificant
and transient. More and more, I longed for the
simplicity of my past life as an archangel, to exist
unfettered by the limitations of mortals.

This yearning reached its apex during the
Lightsong: the creation of new angels. Throngs of
Heaven's denizens gathered at the Crystal Arch, their
essences tuned in synchronicity with the monolithic
structure. From this perfect harmony, angels were
given life. But as a mortal, I could not take part in
this sublime symphony. I could only watch as
the sacred angelic rite unfolded.

I was a stranger in the only place
I had ever called home.

Alienated and apart, I took solace in
my memories of Deckard Cain, of Leah,
and of the nephalem. I looked to them for inspiration.
They had all dealt with adversity and doubt.
They had possessed that wondrous mortal ability to
shape their outlook on the world, to find
hope in despair and muster courage
in the face of overwhelming fear.

I relate this to you, Horadrim, not because I claim my understanding transcends yours. Often, it takes the observation of an outsider to glean true insight about one's self. But if there is one shred of wisdom I can pass on to you, it is that the true strength of mortals comes from the fact that they are forged of equal parts light and dark. From this duality springs a constant push and pull between opposing and contradictory emotions. This shifting spectrum of feeling is what grants mortals their unique perspective and freedom.

Rather than cower from the sudden rush of conflicting emotions, I faced it. I adapted to it. Slowly, I began to see beyond the things that troubled me; I began to glimpse the beauty of Heaven with my new mortal eyes. I marveled at its grandeur, at the way each domain, from the great Halls of Valor to the tranquil Gardens of Hope, had a distinct and profound effect on my mind. I began, at last, to see as mortals do.

It was with this newfound perspective that I first noticed a subtle darkening to the realm of angels. Shadows dimmed the brilliant crystalline spires and colonnades. Discordant notes tainted the radiant chorus that whispered through the skies of the Heavens.

At the center of this growing disharmony, I beheld the Black Soulstone.

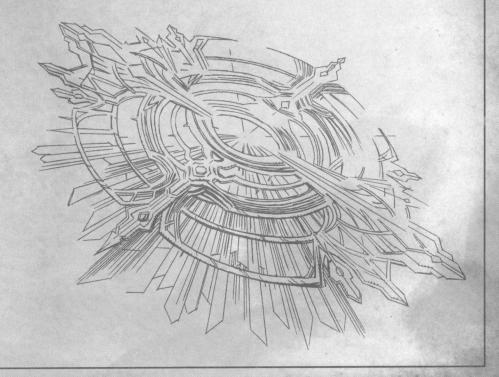

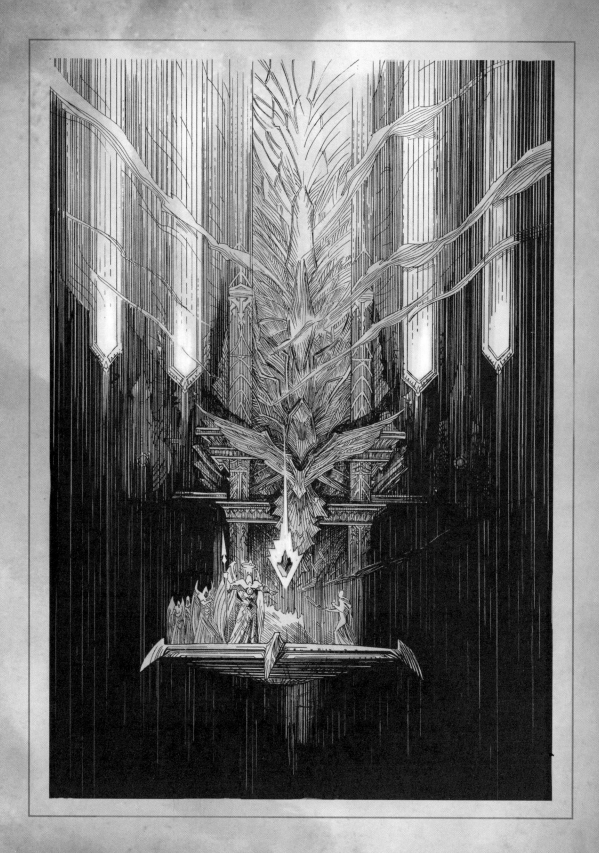

The Dissonance
of the Angiris Council

In the wake of the Prime Evil's defeat, I resumed my involvement with the Angiris Council. Where once I had stood among Heaven's ruling body as the Aspect of Justice, I now assumed the place of Wisdom, a position formerly held by the missing archangel, Malthael. In part, taking on this duty was a deliberate act. I believed that to ensure a new dawn for angels and men, the virtues of wisdom outweighed those of justice. But my transformation was also caused by something more: a subtle calling that emanated from the Crystal Arch, instilling in me a profound need to don the mantle of Wisdom.

Through my involvement with the Council, I was privy to discussions about the Black Soulstone. The Prime Evil's body had been destroyed, but the crystal remained intact, the entity's spirit still roiling within the enchanted prison. Angels under the command of Imperius quickly recovered the foul artifact and entrusted it to the Angiris Council.

Never before had the archangels held such power and dominion over the Lords of the Burning Hells. Never before had they possessed such a momentous chance to purge evil from creation and bring an end to the Eternal Conflict once and for all.

Auriel proposed forging an impenetrable chamber of light and sound to shroud the crystal for all eternity. Imperius argued that the only valid course of action was to shatter the stone, thus destroying the Evil, and launch a final sweeping invasion of the Burning Hells. Itherael lingered in indecision, still plagued by his inability to foresee mankind's destiny in relation to the Prime Evil and the harrowing attack on the Heavens.

The Council was divided, unable to pass a vote on a course of action. It was during these meetings that I began to notice the Black Soulstone's insidious influence on the archangels. This effect was not corruption in the literal sense, although the crystal did possess unsettling powers. Angels who handled it for prolonged periods of time were inundated with visions of terror, hate, destruction, and the other dark emotions intrinsic to the seven Evils. For mortals, I believe this effect would be even more perilous.

The mere presence of the soulstone drove a wedge between the archangels, begetting an unending cycle of heated debates and arguments. Know this: it is harmony that imbues angels with much of their strength. Discord is like a mortal disease that spreads to every limb and organ until the body withers and dies. In that way, the Council's divisiveness pervaded the Heavens, posing a danger to all who dwelt within.

I warned the archangels of this burgeoning schism and the Soulstone's role in it, but I was largely ignored. Imperius took my apprehension as a sign of mortal cowardice. Throughout the Council's meetings, he was loath to hear out any of my suggestions. He continued to hold me accountable for the tragic attack on the Heavens. He also claimed that my nature as a mortal made me incapable of living up to Malthael's legacy as the Aspect of Wisdom.

Imperius's behavior troubled me deeply. Seeing Heaven burn around him, seeing his loyal followers perish before his eyes, had a profound impact on the archangel. Due to his pride, he could not accept that mortals had spared the Heavens from doom. He allowed his shame and anger to feed off one another, blinding him to reason.

There was, however, a shard of truth to his accusations. Although I had willingly become Wisdom, I had not fully embraced my calling. Doubtful that I could live up to Malthael's legacy, I had abstained from bringing other angels under my command. I had even avoided venturing into my predecessor's domain, the Pools of Wisdom, and taking up the legendary source of his power: Chalad'ar, the Chalice of Wisdom.

Would peering into this artifact destroy my mortal mind? Or would it have no effect on me at all? The various outcomes, and the potential for disaster, plagued my thoughts.

I do not believe Imperius intended this, but his constant challenges finally pushed me to face my fears. I knew that as long as the Council remained deadlocked over the Black Soulstone, the dissonance of the archangels would fester like an open wound. Only by drawing on the powers of Wisdom could I hope to resolve this dilemma. So it was that I finally ventured into the Pools of Wisdom to take Chalad'ar into my care.

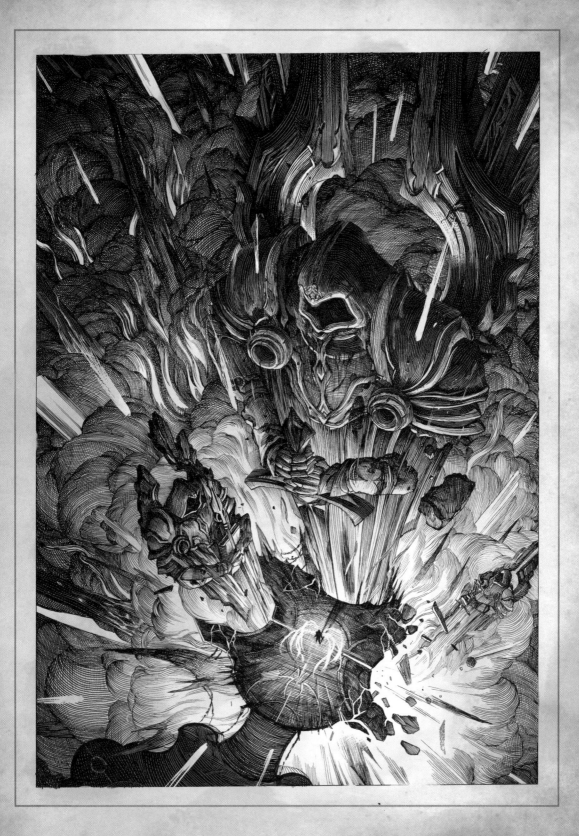

Wisdom

In the long ages after light and sound wove the fabric of the Heavens, Malthael stood as a pillar of reason among the archangels. Whenever disagreement erupted within the Council, he was there to quell the discord, drawing our divergent opinions into perfect harmony. He existed to seek the meaning of all things—the truth in all things.

Despite his great influence, Malthael never forcefully imposed his will on any of the archangels. Quiet and reclusive, he was an enigma to his own kind. Even so, many of Heaven's denizens revered Malthael. Apart from the members of the Angiris Council, throngs of angels frequented the Pools of Wisdom to bask in the tranquil radiance that pervaded the domain. Others lingered there for a chance to engage in discourse with Malthael.

But few were graced with such an opportunity. The archangel of Wisdom rarely spoke. When he did, the chorus of the Heavens would fall silent for the briefest moment and Malthael's words would shine across the realm of angels for all to hear.

When the monolithic Worldstone disappeared in the distant past, Malthael dedicated himself to unraveling the mystery of the crystal's location. But truth proved elusive. The Aspect of Wisdom became increasingly distant and withdrawn from the activities of the Angiris Council. This behavior did not change even after we discovered that the Worldstone had been hidden away on Sanctuary. Malthael continued seeking answers for what this turn of events could mean. For the span of mortal decades, he would sit in silent and frustrated meditation, peering into the mercurial depths of the chalice. The Aspect of Wisdom was also prone to suddenly disappearing from the High Heavens to brood in isolation for lengthy periods of time.

After leaving on one of these mysterious journeys, Malthael simply never returned.

No one knows his current whereabouts. The Council dispatched some of Malthael's closest followers to seek him out, but few ever returned. Rumors persist that he wanders the otherworldly halls of the Pandemonium Fortress, but I have not investigated these reports myself. Whatever the truth may be, the Angiris Council and all of the High Heavens are less without Malthael.

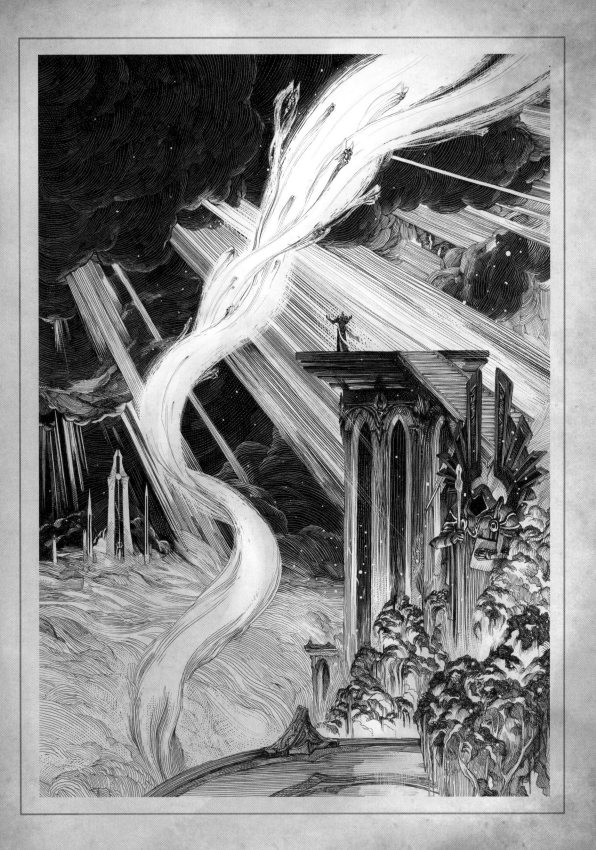

I relay this information here so that you understand the monumental impact my predecessor had on the Heavens. I was concerned that in failing to match Malthael's influence, I would shatter any hopes of bringing angels and humans together. In large part, this mindset is what kept me away from the Pools of Wisdom for so long.

When I finally mustered the courage to venture into Malthael's former home, I found the place cold and desolate, as if it existed just beyond the reach of Heaven's light. An eerie void of sound— a silence almost painful to endure—pervaded the domain. The crystalline cisterns and founts that had once sung with living light had all run dry. It was there, in the silent heart of this formerly glorious realm, that I found Chalad'ar.

What is it like for a mortal to use this vessel of ever-flowing light?

First, know that the chalice was not forged for a mortal mind. Even now, I struggle to tame its energies. Sometimes Chalad'ar awakens the raw power of my mortal emotions, throwing me into states of confusion, fear, and anger. Other times an icy cold surrounds me, chilling my body to the marrow. I become transfixed by the inevitability of my own mortality and of the death that awaits all things.

Of its positive effects, Chalad'ar has many. Staring into the chalice imbues mind and body with a profound sense of confidence, power, and euphoria. It also unravels the barriers of perception, illuminating the interconnectivity of all emotions and ideas, the oneness of all things. Light and dark, love and hate, life and death—to gaze into the chalice is to see that these things are, at their core, merely different facets of the same crystal. In that way, Chalad'ar allows one to perceive situations with flawless objectivity.

Using it confirmed a fear that had been troubling me for some time: so long as the Black Soulstone remained in the care of the archangels, it would bring about the downfall of both the Heavens and the mortal world. The task of standing vigil over the crystal did not lie with the Angiris Council. It lay with mankind. Only humans possessed the potential foresight, willpower, and perspective necessary to take on such a tremendous burden.

As I look back on this revelation, giving the task to mortals seems an obvious solution. But I had hidden from this truth, wanting so much to believe that the Angiris Council possessed the unity to safeguard the soulstone. Chalad'ar stripped away this self-delusion, forcing me to face the stark truth, however painful it was.

Such is the price of wisdom.

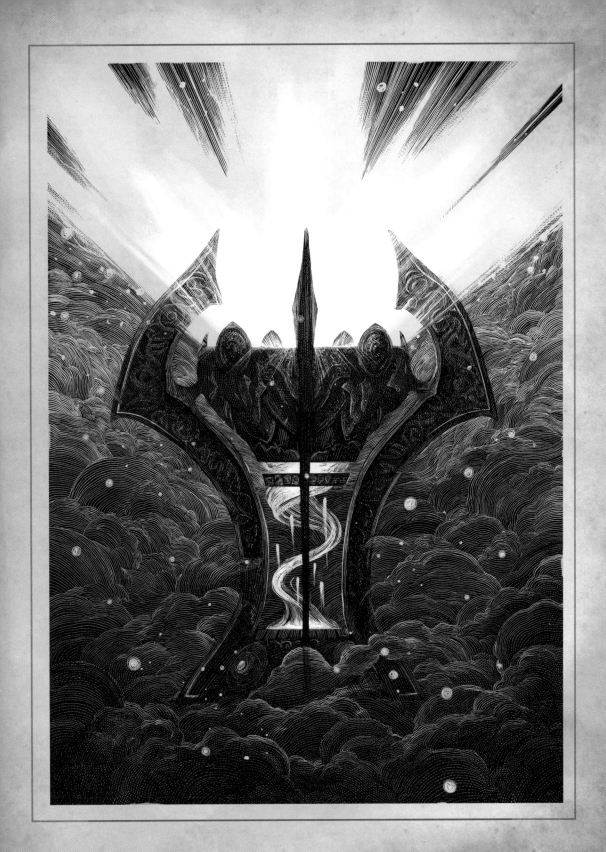

The New Horadrim

I relayed some of the insights I had gleaned from Chalad'ar with the Angiris Council, but it became clear that the archangels would never allow mankind to have dominion over the Black Soulstone. Therefore, I began keeping my thoughts concerning the crystal's fate secret.

As to warriors capable of safeguarding the crystal, I considered many possibilities: the nephalem who had vanquished the Prime Evil, the dedicated and pragmatic priests of Rathma, and the barbarian tribes that had once stood vigil over Mount Arreat with unyielding determination. But always, my thoughts lingered on the first Horadrim.

I will not detail the formation of the original order or their battles against the three Prime Evils. Deckard Cain and others have written extensively on the subject. I will, however, say this: the strength of the Horadrim was their diversity, a virtue lacking in many other mortal organizations. Mages from disparate cultures, some of which were openly hostile toward one another, comprised the order. Although the members constantly bickered and argued, their differences proved to be their greatest weapon. The unique system of belief and worldview held by each of the mages prevented stagnation and allowed them to devise brilliant solutions for the impossible challenges they faced.

But apart from Cain, the Horadrim had ceased to exist centuries ago. Forging another order was a daunting task I did not have the time to undergo. I pushed thoughts of the Horadrim from my mind until I came across this among Cain's writings:

> They call themselves the First Ones.
>
> From what I gathered, a group of scholars stumbled upon a hidden archive of Horadric texts in the city of Gea Kul. A man named Garreth Rau, a litterateur well versed in the arts of magic, assumed leadership of the fledgling order. He and his newfound comrades swore oaths to uphold the tenets of the Horadrim.
>
> Only later was it revealed that Rau had fallen under the sway of Belial, the Lord of Lies. It is unclear precisely when this occurred, but the man sunk into the depths of depravity, engaging in all manner of grotesque blood rituals and human corruption. He also had designs for Leah due to her innate powers, and therefore pulled us both into his web of deception.

Jered Cain, one of the Horadrim's original leaders.

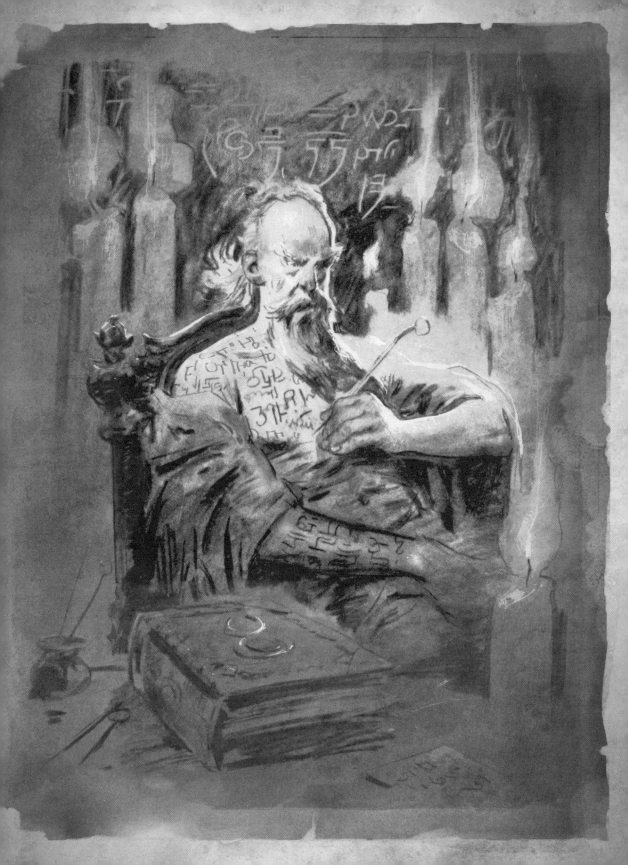

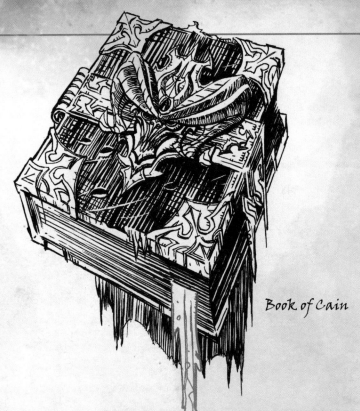

Book of Cain

Quite miraculously, not all of these First Ones darkened as Rau had. There were some who continued to uphold the sanctity of the order through these harrowing events. They were only scholars, but even so they bravely fought to help break Rau's hold over Gea Kul and cleanse the Horadric name of this despicable false leader.

For that, I owe them much. I have nothing but respect for the First Ones, and I have therefore given them my blessing to carry on the Horadric legacy.

Oh, never in my wildest dreams did I imagine the order would rise again. To know that they are out there in the world, upholding the values Archangel Tyrael bestowed on the first Horadrim, fills my heart with joy.

If only I had the time to stand with them. Perhaps someday I will.

iscovering that the order still existed, albeit in a different form than before, invigorated me. These First Ones had laid the foundations of a glorious new Horadrim. With my guidance, I knew they would be the key to guarding the Black Soulstone.

To strengthen the order, I decided to reach out to trustworthy mortals whose talents lay in magic and other martial disciplines. I will not mention their names here, for there are some who may choose not to take part in this perilous endeavor. Know that I hold no ill will toward these individuals. To be Horadrim is to put the lives of others before your own. It is to root out evil in the darkest corners of the world, enduring horrors that would break lesser mortals. Few have the courage to take on this calling.

I was confident in my decision regarding the Horadrim, but the question of where the order could safely watch over the soulstone plagued me. Again, I turned to Cain's writings for answers. I delved into his histories of the secret places of the world: the lost city of Ureh, the Arcane Sanctuary, and many others. I gazed into the shifting depths of Chalad'ar to contemplate everything I had learned and seek insight.

Even now I remain undecided, but thus far a remote network of nephalem catacombs in the kingdom of Westmarch appears most promising. I have included Cain's treatise on this nation's history and its ancient ruins in full should these details prove useful in the future.

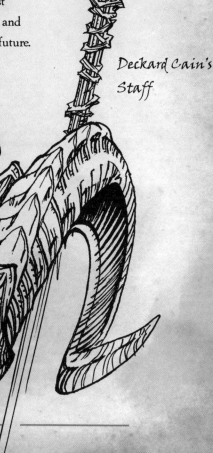

Deckard Cain's
Staff

Tal Rasha's
Guise of Wisdom

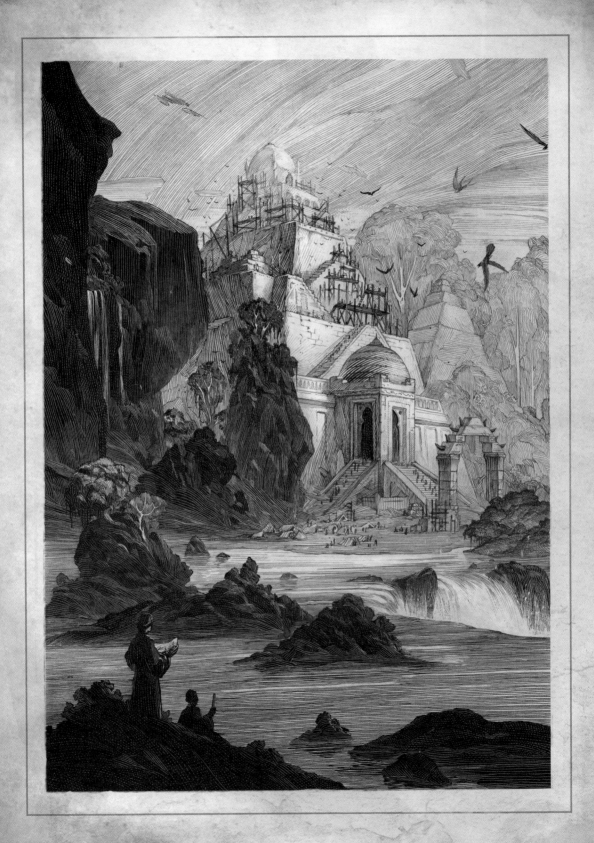

Rakkis and the Founding of Westmarch
Prelude to Conquest

Of all the world's myriad nations, it is Westmarch that has always fascinated me most. I consider this land of rain-soaked ports and sweeping pastures to be one of the greatest kingdoms in existence, a fact made all the more impressive when considering its relatively young age.

But one must remember that the Westmarch of modern times is vastly different from what it was at the moment of its creation. It is this historic event, the founding, which I will examine in some detail here. Much of the information that follows I have taken from *Westmarch and the Sons of Rakkis,* a seminal work on the nation's past.

Let us begin by briefly examining the early days of the Zakarum Church, for this famous institution's rise to power is inexorably linked to the founding of Westmarch.

Nearly three centuries ago, the vast empire of Kehjistan was in the throes of unrest, plagued by famine and disease. Bloody riots between the downtrodden commoners and the corrupt ruling elite were daily occurrences. In short, the climate was ripe for a rebellion by the masses, one on a scale of which Kehjistan had never witnessed.

It was at this rather inauspicious time that the Zakarum, an order that had hitherto existed on the fringes of society, came to prominence. This religion was founded on the teachings of Akarat, a man who wrote of self-determination, empowerment, and the inner Light that exists in every man and woman. It appears that in Kehjistan's state of inequality and hopelessness, the Zakarum tenets blazed across the land like wildfire. Historians also attribute this sudden growth to the building of Travincal, a massive temple complex in Kurast.

Beyond this, I will not delve any further into the Zakarum's rise to power. For the purposes of this story, it is important simply to note that over the course of decades, the church grew increasingly influential, soon becoming a major player in the political spectrum.

Fearful of this burgeoning power, Kehjistan's ruling elite worked to exterminate the Zakarum through acts of violence and persecution. But these brutal tactics only served to drive more of the disillusioned masses into the arms of the church.

It is written that a new emperor by the name of Tassara dismissed this ongoing conflict with the Zakarum as futile. By all accounts, he was a cunning politician and a master of statecraft. Unlike the previous emperor, Tassara did not see the Zakarum as an obstacle. Quite the contrary, he saw it as a means to strengthen his rule.

In a move that is said to have befuddled and infuriated the ruling elite, Tassara converted to the Zakarum faith. He decreed that it would be the official religion of Kehjistan, and he even moved the empire's capital from ancient Viz-jun to Kurast, the headquarters of the church. With this one deft stroke, Tassara won the admiration and, more important, the undying allegiance of Kehjistan's masses.

Westmarch and the Sons of Rakkis states that most of the nobility followed Tassara's lead, but there were some who remained opposed. A handful of nobles had no intention of sharing their power with the church. They pooled their incredible fortunes and recruited a formidable mercenary army to topple Tassara and crush the Zakarum.

This turn of events led the emperor to call upon his greatest military general and lifelong friend: Rakkis. I have found conflicting reports about this man's true origins. What all the histories do agree on, however, is that Rakkis was a zealous Zakarum convert known for his stern demeanor, cunning, and ferocity in battle. Throughout the course of his military career, he gained renown for defending the empire from both external and internal threats.

Most accounts, which I hold true, state that the usurpers' armies outnumbered Rakkis's own forces by a wide margin. Despite this disadvantage, the general outmaneuvered his adversaries at every turn. Indeed, he divided and conquered the mercenaries with incredible speed and efficiency, never losing a single battle.

These victories made Rakkis a legend. Perhaps the masses saw his triumph as a sign of their faith's legitimacy and undeniable strength. Whatever the case, when Rakkis traveled through cities, it is said that people of all ages would gather to catch a glimpse of their champion. The general used his influence to dispose of governors and magistrates whom he saw as inept, replacing them with his favored Zakarum archbishops.

In time, Tassara grew wary of Rakkis's explosive popularity and sought to neutralize this new threat to his rule. The emperor did not, however, turn to violence as a solution. I imagine this was partly due to his friendship with Rakkis. But more important, Tassara knew that eliminating the general would only turn the populace against him.

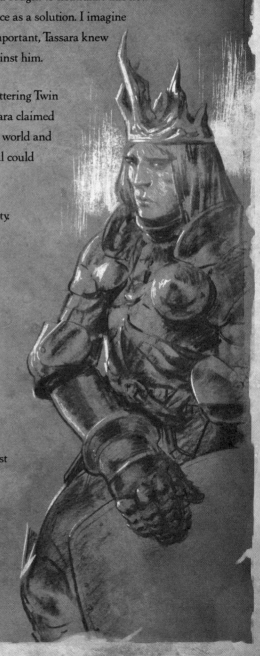

Thus, he took a quite different tactic. To the west, across the glittering Twin Seas, lay untamed and savage lands shrouded in mystery. Tassara claimed that it was the empire's duty to conquer this dark corner of the world and enlighten it with the Zakarum faith, and that only Rakkis's zeal could succeed in doing so.

If the general failed, he would likely lose much of his popularity. If he proved victorious, Tassara would reap the benefits and be seen as the architect of this grand new chapter in Zakarum history. Either way, the emperor would secure a future for himself.

Whether or not Rakkis was aware of Tassara's ulterior motives is unclear, but he accepted the task nonetheless. The emperor granted the general nearly a third of Kehjistan's standing military. This force included many paladins, holy warriors of the Zakarum Church (known as the Protectors of the Word) who used the powers of the Light to smite their foes in battle. Tassara also went to great lengths to ensure that Rakkis's closest allies in the church were included in this bold campaign.

Before thousands of cheering onlookers, the great army set sail in a fleet that, according to one account, stretched from the shores of Kehjistan to the far horizon.

Campaigns Against Ivgorod and the Barbarians

Rakkis first landed in Lut Gholein, an ancient port that had been forewarned of his arrival. The Zakarum faith was already entrenched in the city, having held ties with Kehjistan through trade. Lut Gholein's ruling mercantile guild agreed to supply Rakkis with additional soldiers and provisions in exchange for continued autonomy.

It was outside this city, in the northern reaches of the sun-scorched deserts of Aranoch, where Rakkis would meet his first resistance. The kingdom of Ivgorod controlled vast swaths of the region, although the base of its power lay high in the mountains northwest of the deserts. This ancient culture observed a polytheistic religion vastly different from the Zakarum faith. As such, Ivgorod vehemently opposed Rakkis and his beliefs.

Across the dunes of Aranoch, the two sides clashed in a series of somewhat one-sided engagements. The Kehjistani forces, masters of warfare in open terrain, ultimately crushed their adversaries, thereby shattering Ivgorod's hold on the land. In fact, the victory was so total that the kingdom would never again reclaim the deserts.

Be that as it may, Ivgorod remained a constant thorn in Rakkis's side as he passed over the western Tamoe mountain range. It was there that the Kehjistani soldiers constructed Eastgate Keep, a fortified outpost to defend against their enemy's counterattacks.

Westmarch and the Sons of Rakkis somewhat downplays this portion of the campaign, but I have found other accounts that provide details. Suffice it to say, Rakkis met increasingly fierce resistance in the mountains. It can even be said that Ivgorod intentionally lured the Kehjistani forces farther north into the dense forests and craggy terrain, an environment more suited to the kingdom's style of warfare. Ivgorod's religious rulers also called upon the monks, their greatest and most venerated holy warriors, to strike down the invaders. These incredibly disciplined combatants harassed Rakkis's soldiers at every turn, launching ambushes and covert assaults with devastating results.

It is here that we see the clash of two faiths: paladins trained in the Light battling monks who, it is written, could call upon the gods of the land to imbue themselves with immense power. This was a battle we in the modern times have never truly witnessed.

As the Kehjistani armies continued to spread out into the far north, they met equally fierce resistance from the scattered barbarian tribes around the foothills of Mount Arreat. I can only imagine what it must have been like for the rank-and-file Kehjistani soldiers as they faced these strange and indomitable foes, a people adorned in vivid body paint and screaming savage war cries as they fearlessly charged into battle.

Rakkis would never conquer the barbarians or Ivgorod. Although both of these cultures were deeply wounded by the Kehjistani incursion, they would nonetheless endure.

For the sake of brevity, I will say that the nearby lands of Entsteig and Khanduras both willingly submitted to Rakkis. They did not possess a fraction of the military strength held by Ivgorod or the barbarians. Both Entsteig and Khanduras would accept the Zakarum faith, and in return they would retain much of their independence.

But it was in the south where Rakkis would find his greatest success.

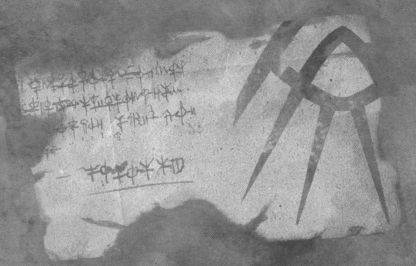

A missive fragment from Rakkis that reads:
". . . northern tribes unyielding. Supplies low.
Request reinforcements from Lut Gholein
with all due haste."

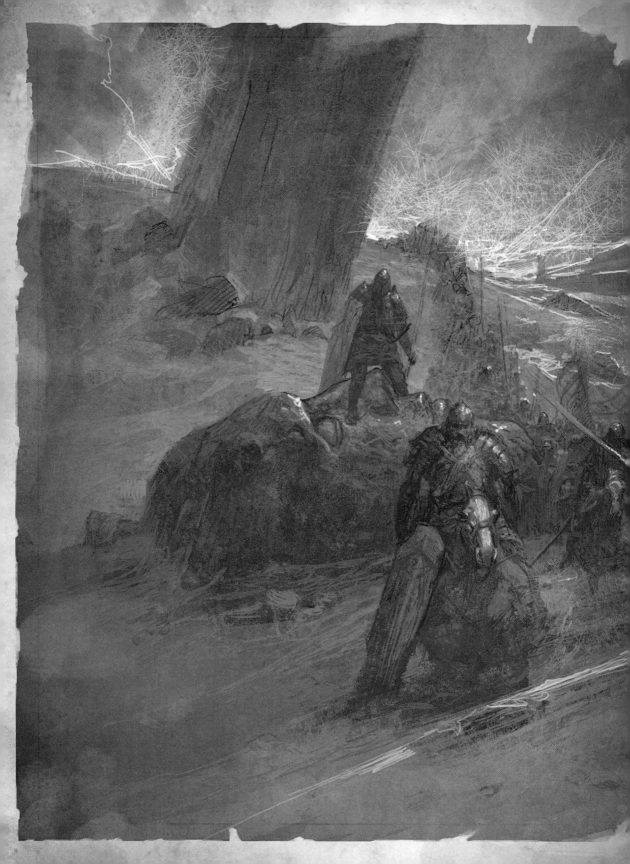

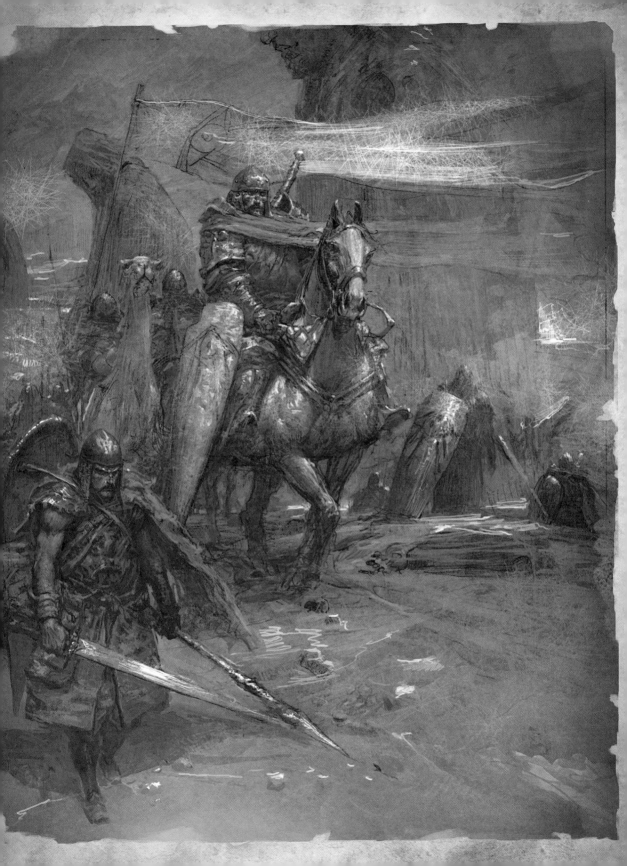

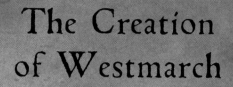

The Creation of Westmarch

Westmarch and the Sons of Rakkis recounts that the general gathered his forces near Eastgate Keep to recuperate and ponder his past defeats. Morale is said to have been low among many of the soldiers following their failed campaigns against Ivgorod and the barbarians. But Rakkis was not dissuaded. As with many of history's conquerors, he believed that victory was his destiny. With speeches about their righteous cause, about their faith's ultimate ascendancy, he rallied his soldiers and set out for the next leg of his campaign.

Nine warring clans existed around the southern edge of what is now called the Gulf of Westmarch. For generations, these hostile peoples had lived in a state of perpetual violence. This disunity was their greatest weakness, and one that Rakkis saw as an advantage. He knew that launching his armies against these clans would inevitably unite them into a single undefeatable force. Instead, Rakkis lived among them. He learned their language and their culture. He learned their gods. All the while he subtly spread the Zakarum faith to all who would hear.

Through an arranged marriage, Rakkis bound himself by blood to the region's third largest clan, the Ortal. He used this new standing as leverage, bringing four of the lesser clans under his banner.

Rakkis then launched his combined forces in a full assault against the largest and most hostile clan, the Hathlan. It is difficult for my mind to fully grasp the terrible nature of the battles that followed. Sources state that blood turned the once verdant fields to marshland. The stench of decaying corpses carried on the wind as far as Khanduras.

At the Battle of Dyre River, the Kehjistani forces dismantled the tattered remnants of the Hathlan army and slew its leader. This clan, in addition to the three others that had abstained from taking a side, quickly submitted to Rakkis's rule. The people of the gulf, having witnessed the general's supremacy, declared him their one true king.

But even as Rakkis assumed dominion over his new subjects, he rallied them with talk of mankind's inner Light and glory. It was his unyielding strength and conviction that truly united these formerly intractable peoples and forged them into a single proud kingdom.

In honor of his long and grueling campaign to spread the faith from distant Kehjistan, Rakkis named his territory Westmarch. Its borders stretched from the gulf to the Great Ocean. For the capital (which would come to share the same name as the kingdom), Rakkis ordered the construction of a river port settlement. The subsequent years saw Westmarch flourish. New roads, cities, and infrastructure sprouted up throughout the land. Due to plentiful access to the sea, the nation quickly became a formidable naval and mercantile power.

Rakkis ruled with a strong but fair hand and enjoyed the admiration of his people. Years after founding his nation, he would launch further incursions against the barbarians, but he would never make any true gains against the fierce northern tribes. It is said that Rakkis died peacefully in his sleep over the age of one hundred. His legacy would continue long after his death. Indeed, Westmarch's current standing in the world is a testament to the dedication and wisdom that he employed to build a nation.

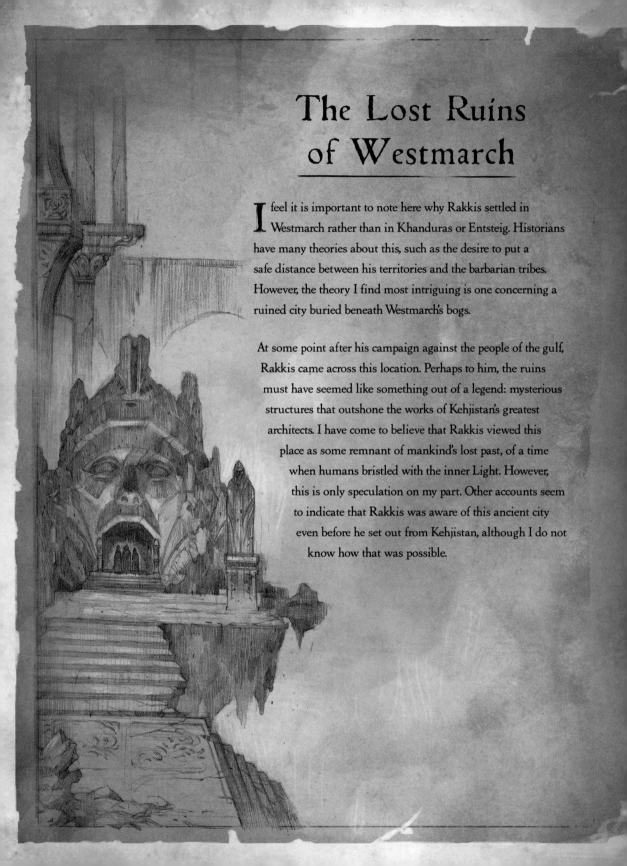

The Lost Ruins of Westmarch

I feel it is important to note here why Rakkis settled in Westmarch rather than in Khanduras or Entsteig. Historians have many theories about this, such as the desire to put a safe distance between his territories and the barbarian tribes. However, the theory I find most intriguing is one concerning a ruined city buried beneath Westmarch's bogs.

At some point after his campaign against the people of the gulf, Rakkis came across this location. Perhaps to him, the ruins must have seemed like something out of a legend: mysterious structures that outshone the works of Kehjistan's greatest architects. I have come to believe that Rakkis viewed this place as some remnant of mankind's lost past, of a time when humans bristled with the inner Light. However, this is only speculation on my part. Other accounts seem to indicate that Rakkis was aware of this ancient city even before he set out from Kehjistan, although I do not know how that was possible.

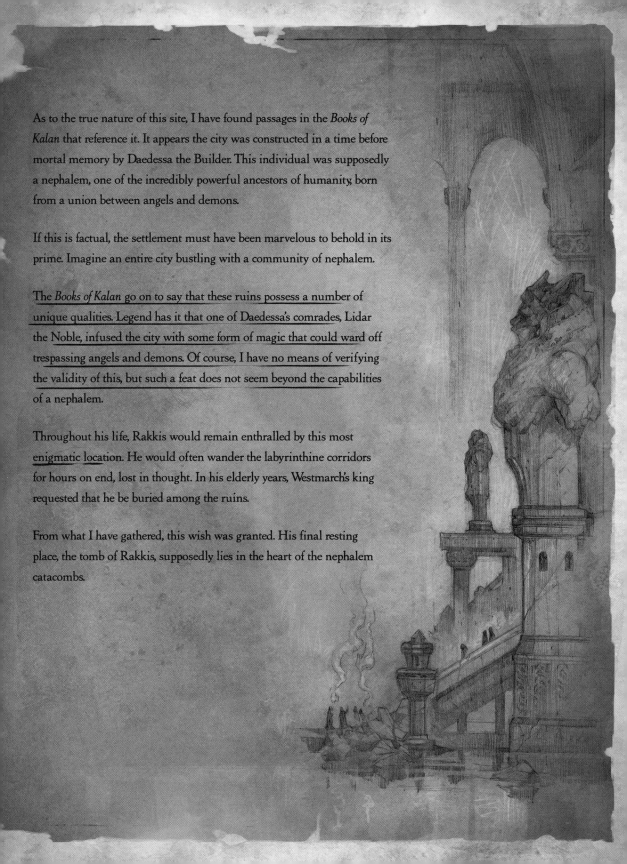

As to the true nature of this site, I have found passages in the *Books of Kalan* that reference it. It appears the city was constructed in a time before mortal memory by Daedessa the Builder. This individual was supposedly a nephalem, one of the incredibly powerful ancestors of humanity, born from a union between angels and demons.

If this is factual, the settlement must have been marvelous to behold in its prime. Imagine an entire city bustling with a community of nephalem.

The *Books of Kalan* go on to say that these ruins possess a number of unique qualities. Legend has it that one of Daedessa's comrades, Lidar the Noble, infused the city with some form of magic that could ward off trespassing angels and demons. Of course, I have no means of verifying the validity of this, but such a feat does not seem beyond the capabilities of a nephalem.

Throughout his life, Rakkis would remain enthralled by this most enigmatic location. He would often wander the labyrinthine corridors for hours on end, lost in thought. In his elderly years, Westmarch's king requested that he be buried among the ruins.

From what I have gathered, this wish was granted. His final resting place, the tomb of Rakkis, supposedly lies in the heart of the nephalem catacombs.

Crusaders

As an addendum to the story of Westmarch, I find it prudent to touch on a separate campaign launched in the name of the Zakarum faith. Whereas Rakkis had gone west, seeking conquest, this other force had gone east, driven by entirely different motivations.

The following information comes from a number of distinct (and sometimes contradictory) sources. However, I am confident the details herein are in large part factual.

Around the time that Rakkis began his historic march, a Zakarum cleric grew troubled by what he saw as a subtle darkening of the church. This man, named Akkhan, was of the belief that the faithful had strayed dangerously far from Akarat's original tenets.

What was this "darkening" he became aware of? I can only assume it was related to the Sapphire Soulstone, the enchanted crystal that contained Mephisto, the Lord of Hatred. At the Horadrim's request, the Zakarum had taken this vile artifact, vowing to safeguard it. They stayed true to their word, but Mephisto's influence nonetheless began seeping into the hearts and minds of the church's spiritual leaders.

Whether or not the cleric knew of the corruption's precise source is unclear. Regardless, Akkhan acted to forestall the faith's impending doom. I take the following from the scrolls of Sarjuq, a text of rare and little-known Zakarum history:

> Akkhan searched far and wide for warriors of unparalleled strength, for believers who burned with an inner Light that was blinding to behold. He made them, these men and women whom fate pulled to his side like iron to the lodestone, into crusaders.

It is said that the cleric gave these crusaders a seemingly impossible task: to scour the far-flung lands to the east and find a means, however it might manifest, to purify the Zakarum faith.

The Book of Cain explores the Zakarum's stewardship of Mephisto's soulstone in greater detail.

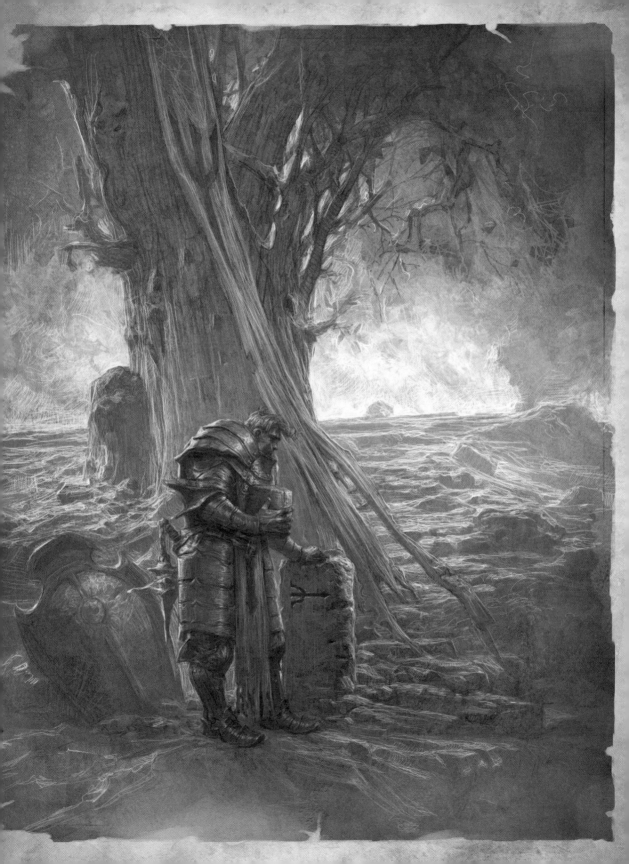

It is important to note that the members of this order were not paladins. Akkhan specifically avoided calling on those individuals because he saw them as a product of the church's errant ways. No, crusaders were a different breed of holy warrior. Resourceful and resilient, they were trained to wield powers unlike any before.

After rigorous preparations, the crusaders fanned out into the east, each one going a separate way. They lived off the land, never staying in settled places for longer than necessary. They developed secret symbols and hand gestures to communicate with other crusaders whom, by chance, they might cross paths with. Every firsthand account I have found concerning these individuals depicts them with an air of mystery.

But herein lies something of a puzzle, for I have also heard tales that the crusaders made no effort to mask their presence. It is even rumored they spoke openly about their sacred quest to anyone with the courage to ask.

On the topic of crusader succession, it seems that they chose a single initiate to train and mentor in their ways. These individuals, recruited from local populations, were picked based on a number of factors, such as their innate affinity to Akarat's teachings.

It is worth mentioning that becoming a member of the order was not without its sacrifices. Initiates were asked to expunge every vestige of their former lives forever. When their mentor perished, the acolytes would take on their master's identity, donning his or her weaponry, armor, and even name. Only then did these initiates ascend to the rank of crusader themselves.

Of the order's mission, I am woefully lacking in details. It appears that some crusaders investigated legends of lost Zakarum writings and holy relics from bygone eras. Others were driven by stories of infants born with an inner Light so pure that it would cleanse the faith of its affliction. But I have found no definitive evidence that states a crusader actually uncovered a means to complete his or her quest.

What I do know is that the crusaders exhausted most—if not all—promising leads in the east. Over two centuries after beginning their search, members of the order began returning to Kehjistan. Their names, beliefs, and sacred mission were the same, but they were a different people, born of the rugged cultures at the edge of the known world.

It is tragic (or perhaps timely) that they returned to Kehjistan when they did. The Zakarum Church had already succumbed to demonic corruption. Travincal and the surrounding city of Kurast had transformed into a cauldron of banditry and suffering.

This, it seems, was precisely the state of affairs Akkhan had warned of. For the crusaders, I imagine that seeing the ailing condition of the Zakarum faith only strengthened their sense of purpose in life.

From what I have gathered, the remaining crusaders are now fixing their gazes to the unplumbed lands of the west to continue their search with even greater voracity.

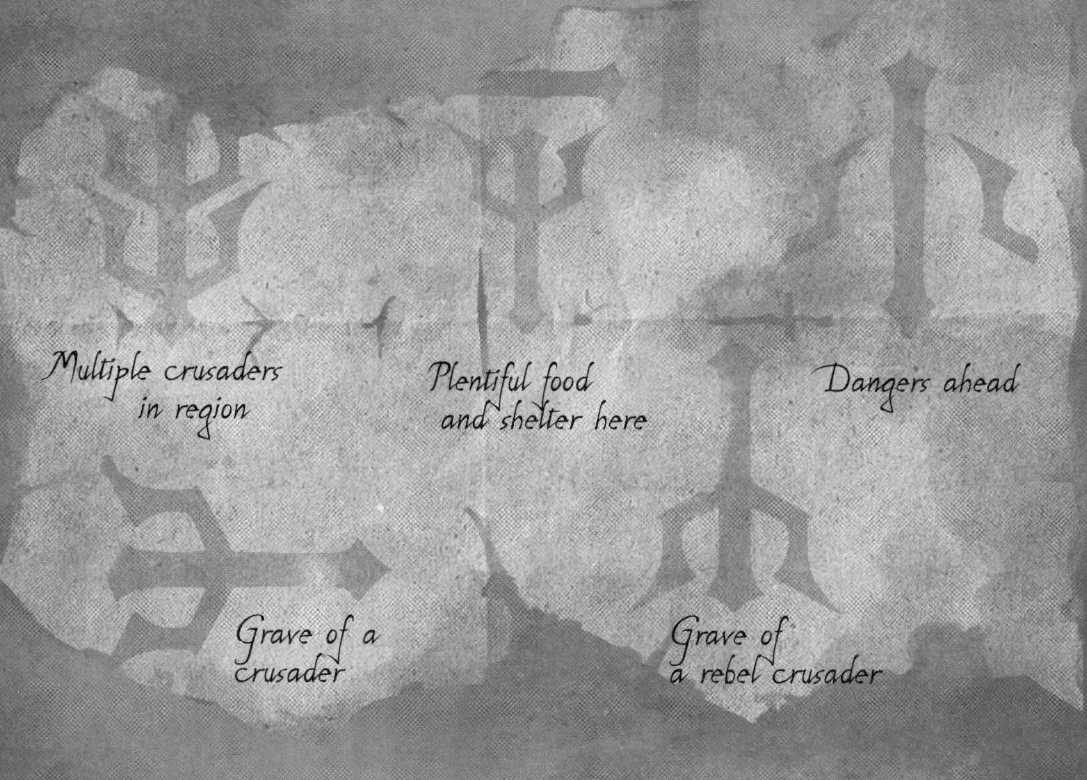

Multiple crusaders in region

Plentiful food and shelter here

Dangers ahead

Grave of a crusader

Grave of a rebel crusader

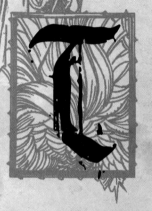

Part Three
Miscellanea

he following comes from the tomes of Deckard Cain. These pages document a broad spectrum of information, from mortal history to the powerful individuals who inhabit the world. Pay heed to everything, Horadrim, for even the most unassuming details may be useful in the days ahead. Knowledge is one of the order's greatest weapons. Wield it carefully.

A Timeline of Sanctuary

At the apex of Zakarum power, the church gathered a veritable army of scholars to document the history of the world as they saw it. I have used this seminal work as the bones from which to build my own timeline, correcting errors as well as removing and adding dates (such as in the pre-history below). Dear reader, keep in mind that this is history at the briefest of glances, a mere tool for understanding whence we have come and where the intertwining paths of fate and destiny may lead us in the future.

Pre-History

The following is based on the apocryphal writings of sages and madmen. After much consideration and scrutiny, I feel this account represents an accurate depiction of the epochs that lay beyond the reach of mortal memory.

Anu and the Dragon

Before time, before even the universe as we know it existed, there was only Anu, the One. This single crystalline entity encompassed all things, including good and evil. Longing for a harmony of essence, it expelled every dissonant and dark aspect of itself. These impurities coalesced into the embodiment of pure evil: Tathamet, the seven-headed dragon.

Within their womb of reality, Anu and Tathamet clashed in a spectacular battle that strained the very fabric of creation. Their final blows sparked an incredible explosion, a cataclysm so violent that it destroyed both beings and birthed the physical universe. This event is something I am afraid a mortal mind will never truly fathom.

The blast left behind an eternal scar called Pandemonium. At the center of this otherworldly realm sat the Worldstone, a monolithic crystal said to be the Eye of Anu.

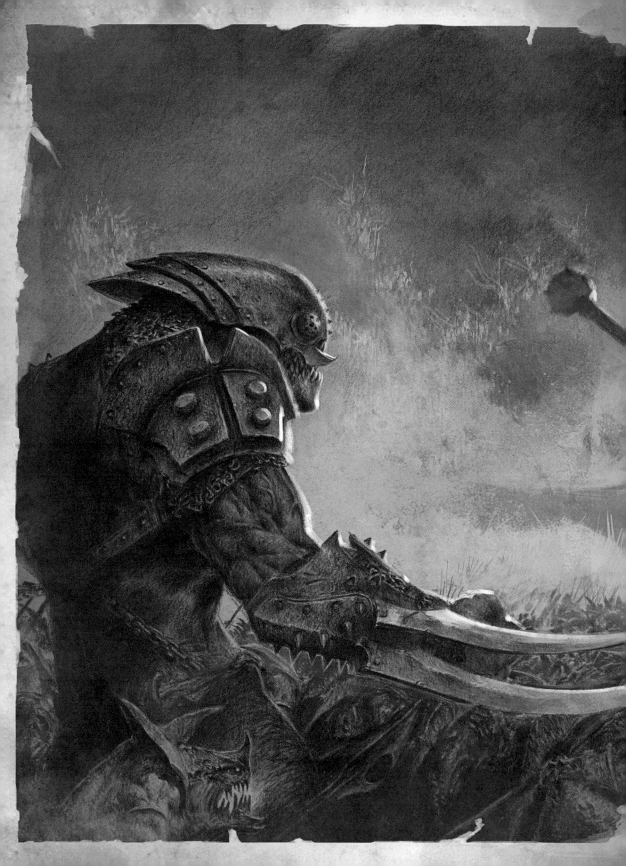

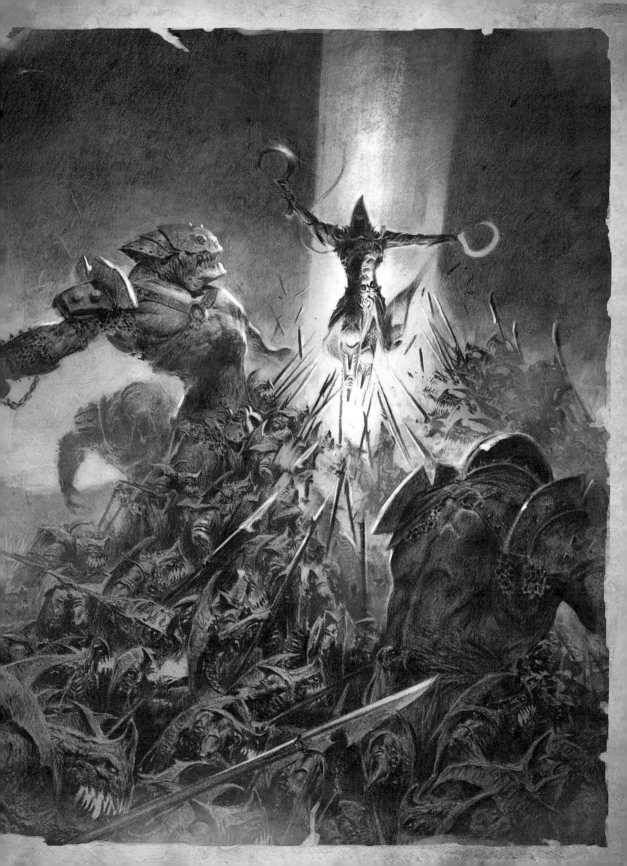

The High Heavens and the Burning Hells

Anu's fragmented spine careened through the infant universe. This remnant of the One became the Crystal Arch, around which the High Heavens thrummed into existence. The Arch resonated life itself, conceiving pulses of sentient energies called angels. The manifestations of Anu's purest aspects—archangels—formed the Angiris Council to govern the brilliant expanses of the Heavens. The members of this ruling body are:

> *Imperius, the Aspect of Valor*
> *Tyrael, the Aspect of Justice*
> *Auriel, the Aspect of Hope*
> *Malthael, the Aspect of Wisdom*
> *Itherael, the Aspect of Fate*

Tathamet's desiccated corpse spiraled through the darkest folds of reality. The Burning Hells manifested from his smoldering body. Demons, in all their forms, were birthed from the Dragon's rotting flesh. Tathamet's seven heads became the seven Evils:

THE PRIME EVILS	*THE LESSER EVILS*
Mephisto, the Lord of Hatred	*Azmodan, the Lord of Sin*
Baal, the Lord of Destruction	*Belial, the Lord of Lies*
Diablo, the Lord of Terror	*Duriel, the Lord of Pain*
	Andariel, the Maiden of Anguish

The Eternal Conflict Begins

From the very moment of their existence, the High Heavens and the Burning Hells clashed in the Eternal Conflict, an apocalyptic war for dominion over all creation. Although the tide of battle ebbed and flowed over the millennia, the war itself was never-ending.

We must understand here that both the High Heavens and the Burning Hells desired complete control of the Worldstone, for it was with this most miraculous artifact that angels and demons had the power to forge worlds in their image. As such, the majority of the Eternal Conflict raged in the twisted heart of Pandemonium. It is said that ownership of the crystal has changed innumerable times over the eons of battle.

The Creation of Sanctuary

As the eons passed, an angel named Inarius grew disillusioned with the Eternal Conflict. Indeed, he saw the war itself as unjust. Thus, he gathered like-minded angels and, shockingly, even demons to his side. Inarius then altered the frequency of the Worldstone, thrusting the crystal into a parallel reality and shrouding it from the eyes of the Heavens and the Hells. There, the renegade angels and demons created Sanctuary, a wondrous paradise world where they could spend eternity in peace.

Birth of the Nephalem

In a most unprecedented act, angels and demons commingled, siring offspring called the nephalem. Born of light and dark, these beings had the potential to become even mightier than their progenitors. In fact, the nephalem were so powerful that Inarius and his comrades feared they might upset the balance of the Eternal Conflict and wreak havoc across the universe.

So it was that the angels and demons debated the fate of their beloved children. Some of them (at one time, even Inarius) considered exterminating the nephalem.

The Purge

Inarius's mate, the demoness Lilith, grew horrified at the thought of losing her offspring. In a fit of ruthless fury, she hunted down the other renegades and slaughtered them one by one. Only Inarius and the nephalem were spared from her fearsome wrath.

Shocked by Lilith's deeds, Inarius banished her from Sanctuary. He could not, however, bring himself to harm the innocent nephalem. He attuned the Worldstone so that it would cause their powers to diminish over time. According to legend, Inarius then disappeared into the wilds of Sanctuary and was not seen again for millennia.

An unknown span of time passed after this series of events. We can assume generations of nephalem lived and died. With their powers dampened and their life spans decreased, they became mortals, completely ignorant of their incredible heritage.

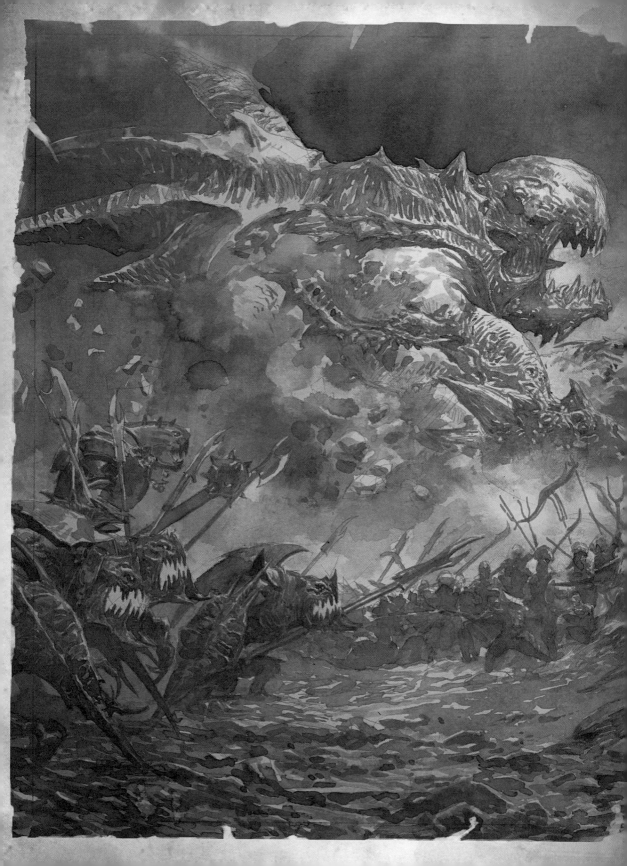

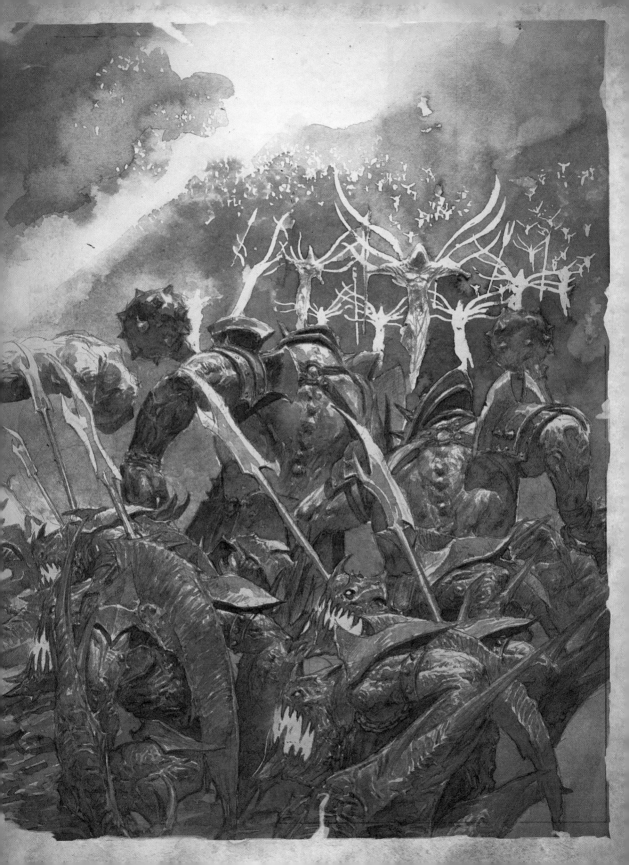

Recorded History

Circa —2300 Anno Kehjistani—The Dawn of Civilization

Recovered tablets, pottery fragments, and other artifacts indicate that writing, art, and science had by this time become an integral part of humanity's culture. The majority of scholars, myself included, agree that this date marks the rise of the first great human civilization. This kingdom was known as Kehjan (now modern-day Kehjistan).

Circa —2200 Anno Kehjistani— Formation of the Mage Clans

Records show that the cultures around Kehjan formalized the study of the arcane sciences. This in turn led to the formation and growth of numerous mage clans.

How many of these clans existed remains something of a mystery, but it should be noted that the Vizjerei would make the largest impact on history in the centuries to come. This clan's school of thought revolved around the arts of conjuring, summoning, and communing with spirits.

Circa —2100 Anno Kehjistani— Ascendancy of the Mage Clans

The increasingly powerful mage clans became a fixture in Kehjan's government. An organization composed of members from each of the major clans—the Al'Raqish, or Mage Council—was formed to rule alongside the kingdom's monarchy and trade guilds.

—1992 Anno Kehjistani—Sanctuary Revealed

Overcome with frustration and rage at the loss of his family, a little-known Vizjerei sorcerer named Jere Harash summoned the first demon into Sanctuary. His fellow mage clan members quickly perfected this dark art, establishing demonology and the enslavement of Hell's minions as the basis of their power.

Of greater importance, however, is that Harash's act alerted the Burning Hells to Sanctuary's existence. It was at this terrible moment when the Prime Evils learned of mankind and its potential to be used as a weapon against the Heavens. Thereafter, the Lords of the Burning Hells began formulating a devious plan to corrupt humanity.

Mark this date well, dear reader. Nearly all things that come afterward are, at least in some small way, a consequence of Harash's reckless summoning.

—1880 Anno Kehjistani—The Temple of the Triune

The influence of the Prime Evils pervaded the lands of Kehjan through a seemingly noble organization: the Temple of the Triune. This cult was based on the worship of three benevolent deities (who, in fact, were actually the three Prime Evils in subtle guises). The Triune posited that through selfless worship and devotion, the cult's wondrous deities could improve life. In time, the religion's numbers swelled.

—1820 Anno Kehjistani— The Veiled Prophet and the Cathedral of Light

Inarius, assuming the identity of a figure named the Prophet, emerged to combat the Triune's burgeoning influence. To do so, he formed a separate faith called the Cathedral of Light. This religion was founded on the tenets of tolerance, cooperation, and unity.

In time, both the Cathedral of Light and the Triune achieved immense influence over the people of Kehjan.

—1809 Anno Kehjistani—The Sin War

An ideological battle between the followers of the Triune and the Cathedral of Light erupted, polarizing Kehjani society. So began what is known as the Sin War.

Understand that this was no mere religious struggle. The entire conflict was a proxy war between the Prime Evils and Inarius for the very souls of mankind.

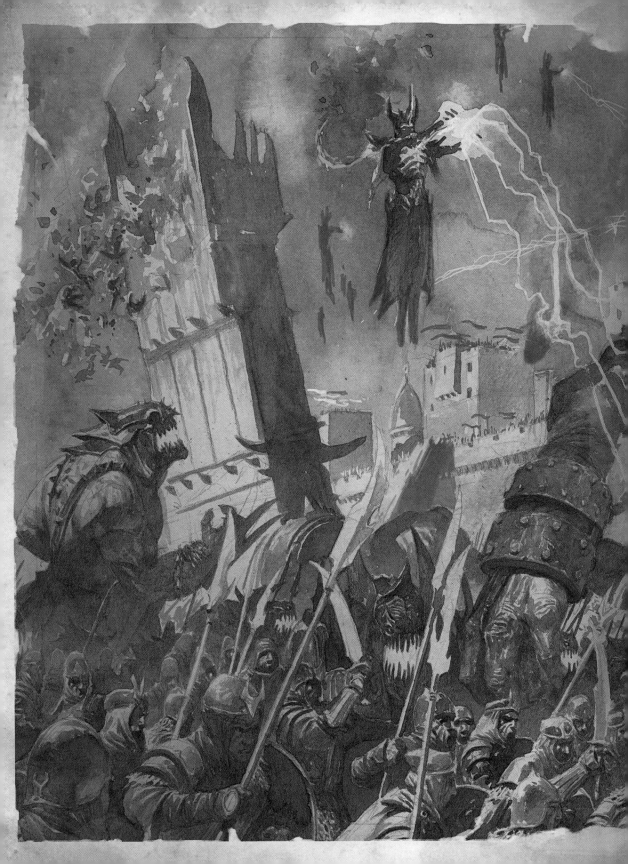

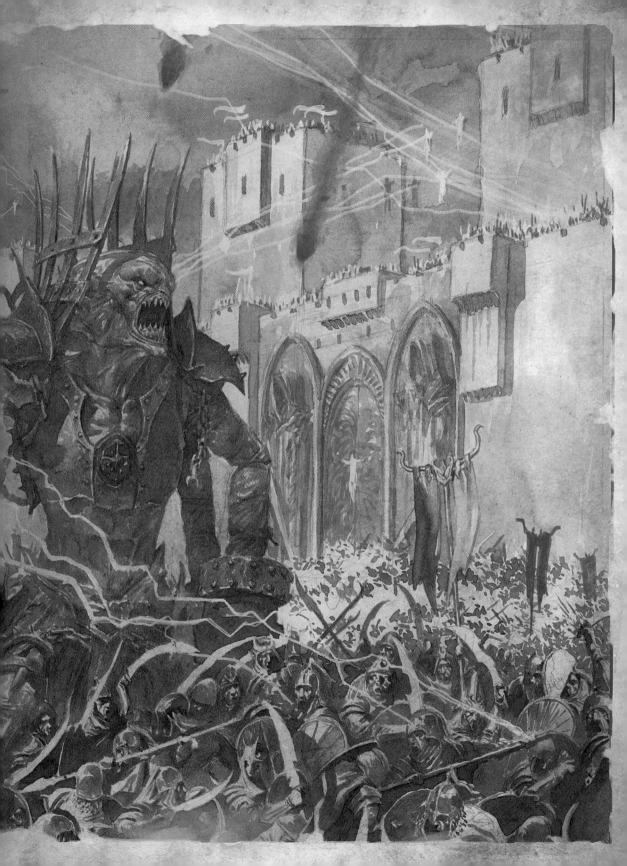

Unbeknownst to either the Prime Evils or Inarius, the demoness Lilith had returned to Sanctuary to protect her children from the Triune and the Cathedral of Light. She awakened the nephalem powers in a man named Uldyssian ul-Diomed, who went on to do the same for other humans. These individuals—called the edyrem—waged war against the Triune and the Cathedral of Light, for they saw both organizations as the source of Kehjan's strife.

These battles proved catastrophic, drawing armies from the Burning Hells and the High Heavens to the mortal world. Uldyssian unleashed the full fury of his might, driving back the invading armies of angels and demons. But in doing so, he also realized that the untamed nephalem energies were threatening to destroy the world. So it was that he sacrificed his life to re-attune the Worldstone, thereby ridding humans of their budding nephalem powers.

It is vital to note here that the Heavens deliberated on mankind's ultimate fate. The final vote, cast by Archangel Tyrael, is what spared us from extermination. Following this, the angels brokered an unlikely truce with the Lords of the Hells. In summation, both sides agreed that they would not further interfere with the lives of humans.

The memories of the edyrem were then erased, and lies were crafted to hide the truth of the nephalem, angels, and demons from the rest of mankind. But some would remain aware of the dark era that was the Sin War. It is through their stories, passed down from generation to generation, that we know the truth of this catastrophic conflict.

What of Lilith? During the war, Inarius had again banished her from Sanctuary. I have seen no evidence of her return. As for Inarius, the angels gave him to the Prime Evils as part of the pact between Heaven and Hell. It is said he suffered eternal torment thereafter.

—1799 Anno Kehjistani—The Golden Age of Magic

Believing that the Sin War was merely a clash of faiths, the majority of Kehjan's populace turned away from religion. Indeed, the people even went so far as to rename Kehjan to Kehjistan as a means to distance themselves from the terrible conflict.

More and more, the people looked to the mage clans for guidance, for they had always placed reason and practical research above all else. A golden age of magic and enlightenment unfolded, an age of wonders unlike anything the world had yet seen.

Certain members of the clans remained aware of the truth behind the Sin War, and rules and regulations were imposed that strictly forbade the art of demonology.

—264 Anno Kehjistani—Prelude to the Mage Clan Wars

This golden age waned when the other mage clans came to a chilling discovery: the Vizjerei sorcerers were continuing the outlawed practice of demonology. This revelation sparked a series of covert assassinations and political intrigue aimed at stripping the Vizjerei of their power. These machinations slowly ate away at the heart of the mage clans.

—210 Anno Kehjistani—The Mage Clan Wars

Following an increase in hostilities between the mages, bloodshed erupted in the streets of Kehjistan's major cities. This violent tide surged into an all-out war pitting the Vizjerei against their rival clans. It is said that spectacular battles flared across the kingdom as the era's preeminent mages unleashed the full fury of their powers against one another.

—203 Anno Kehjistani—Bartuc and Horazon

Pushed to the brink of annihilation by the other clans, the Vizjerei unleashed their last desperate weapon: demons. Wielding the minions of Hell, the sorcerers obliterated their enemies, driving them back behind the walls of the empire's ancient capital, Viz-jun.

It was then that disaster struck. The Vizjerei's Ruling Council dismissed one of its most formidable members, Bartuc, for acts of depravity. This infamous figure, also known as the Warlord of Blood, turned against his own clan and ignited civil war.

A terrible battle ensued between the sundered halves of the Vizjerei clan at the gates of Viz-jun. Bartuc's brother, Horazon, emerged to strike down his ruthless sibling. Although he succeeded in vanquishing the Warlord of Blood, the cost was unimaginable. The battle reduced the capital to smoldering rubble, killing tens of thousands in the process.

So ended this dark and terrible conflict. So ended the reign of the mage clans. Broken by the wars, they would never again rise to such heights of power and glory.

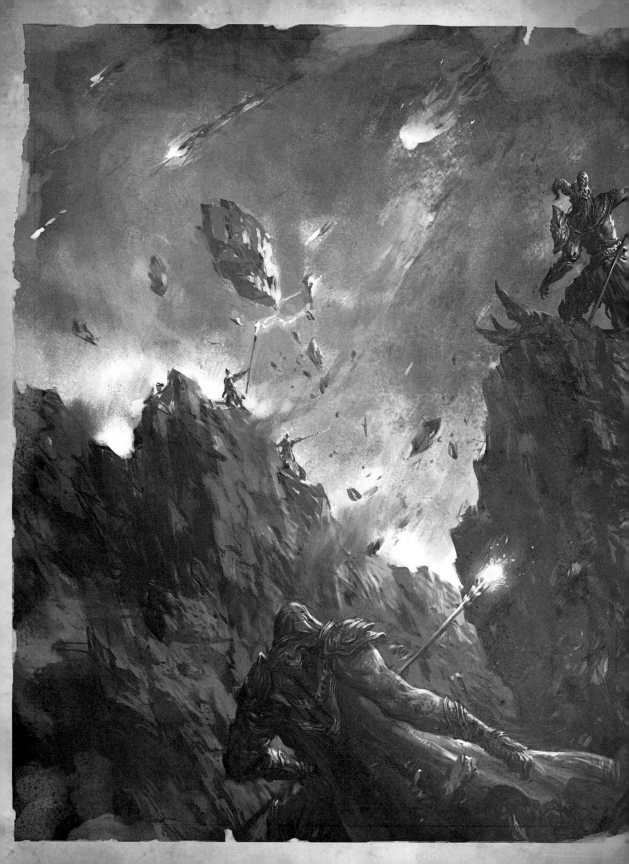

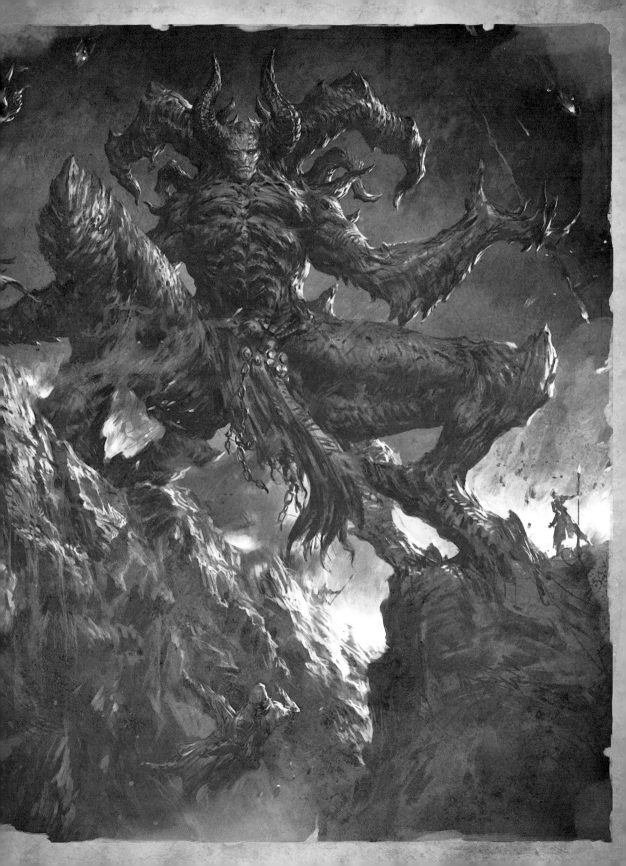

0 Anno Kehjistani—Akarat and the Zakarum Faith

The untold death and suffering wrought during the Mage Clan Wars pushed mankind away from the arcane sciences. The passage of centuries saw humans once again explore faith and religion as a source of meaning and purpose. A number of religious figures arose during this era, but there is one in particular who merits attention: Akarat.

In the mountains of Xiansai, this wandering ascetic saw visions of what he claimed to be the angel Yaerius. From this encounter, Akarat formulated his ideas about the inner Light within all humans. Every man and woman, he claimed, was bound together in a spectrum of cosmic radiance that was the foundation of existence itself.

His ideas formed the core tenets of what would become known as the Zakarum faith. Akarat spread his teachings and garnered the support of a small band of followers, but for the next thousand years, his philosophies would flounder in obscurity.

964 Anno Kehjistani—The Dark Exile

Believing the Prime Evils had abandoned the Eternal Conflict in favor of corrupting humanity, the Lesser Evils waged a catastrophic war against their superiors. The uprising, led by Azmodan and Belial, rocked the Burning Hells to the core. Following a violent series of engagements, the usurpers banished the Prime Evils to Sanctuary.

I often wonder how Diablo and his brethren reacted upon reaching the mortal realm. It is entirely possible that, for a time, they cursed their fates. However, I am of the belief that the Prime Evils quickly saw their exile as an unexpected and fortuitous chance to corrupt the hearts of mankind. So it was that they began turning brother against brother and nation against nation, fomenting unrest throughout Kehjistan.

1004–1010 Anno Kehjistani—The Hunt for the Three

Having secretly watched the mortal world for centuries, Archangel Tyrael learned of the Prime Evils and their machinations. Understand, dear reader, that he did not directly oppose the demons, for he feared his actions would alert the Heavens to what was transpiring on Sanctuary. Tyrael knew that if such an event occurred, the angels might very well decide to exterminate mankind once and for all. And so Tyrael forged the Horadrim to serve as his hand in the mortal world, a secret order composed of members from the disparate mage clans.

Tyrael bestowed upon the Horadrim three crystalline soulstones (supposedly cleaved from the Worldstone itself). He tasked the great mages with a perilous mission: to hunt down the Prime Evils and imprison them within the recesses of the soulstones.

First, the mages captured Mephisto in one of Kehjistan's sprawling urban centers. The demon's Sapphire Soulstone was given to the humble Zakarum order for safekeeping.

Next, the Horadrim harried Baal and Diablo across the Twin Seas and into the western lands. In the deserts of Aranoch, they confronted the Lord of Destruction. Although the mages prevailed against the demon, Baal's Amber Soulstone was left shattered.

The order's leader, Tal Rasha, selflessly used his own body to contain the Lord of Destruction's raging essence. So it was that, with heavy hearts, the Horadrim sealed away their noble leader within a subterranean tomb.

In the wake of this tragedy, Jered Cain took leadership of the bruised and battered mages. Together, the Horadrim struck out to imprison the last of the Prime Evils: Diablo.

1017 Anno Kehjistani—The Building of Travincal

The Zakarum began constructing Travincal, a fortified temple complex in Kurast that would house Mephisto's wretched soulstone. The enormous undertaking brought sudden notoriety to the order and sparked immense interest in Zakarum teachings. Indeed, in a matter of months, throngs of Kehjistan's downtrodden masses flocked to Travincal to lend their aid. It is rumored that the temple's construction was finished in just over a year.

In hindsight, it is easy to see why interest in the faith took hold so quickly. Corruption and intolerance had eaten away at the foundations of society, and the common folk found inspiration and hope in the Zakarum's tenets of self-empowerment and equality.

1019 Anno Kehjistani—The Fall of Diablo

Led by Jered Cain, the Horadrim tracked Diablo to Khanduras and defeated him in a battle that nearly cost them their lives. They buried the Lord of Terror's Crimson Soulstone in a labyrinthine cave system near the river Talsande. The Horadrim who remained in Khanduras (including Jered) built a small monastery and a network of catacombs over the burial spot.

1025 Anno Kehjistani — The Founding of Tristram

The Horadrim in Khanduras settled the land near their monastery and founded the quaint village of Tristram. In the years that followed, the town attracted farmers and settlers from the surrounding region.

1042 Anno Kehjistani — Rise of the Zakarum Church

Despite the capture of the Prime Evils, Kehjistani society remained in a dire state, plagued by famine and disease. Commoners increasingly viewed the ruling elite as the cause of their ills. Rebellion was poised to tear the empire asunder.

It was at this critical point that a new Kehjistani emperor, Tassara, converted to the populist (and increasingly influential) Zakarum faith. In doing so, he gained the adoration of the masses and strengthened his hold over the region.

Zakarum became the dominant religion in Kehjistan. The empire's capital was moved from ancient Viz-jun to Kurast. Tassara worked to codify the faith's beliefs and elect the first Que-Hegan—the highest divine authority of the religion. At this date we begin to see records describing Zakarum in terms of an organized and structured church.

Over the next three years, Tassara's budding popularity was overshadowed by that of his childhood friend: the famous military general and zealous Zakarum convert Rakkis. After defeating a group of renegade nobles who sought to overthrow the church, the general became a legend among the masses. It is said that Rakkis used his burgeoning influence to replace government officials with Zakarum archbishops, thereby upsetting the balance of power in the region.

1045 Anno Kehjistani — Rakkis and the Western Campaign

Wary of Rakkis's growing popularity, Emperor Tassara dispatched the general on a grand mission to spread the Zakarum faith to the untamed lands of the west. Once the general and his most loyal forces had gone, the emperor secured his dominion over Kehjistan.

1045 Anno Kehjistani—
The Crusaders and the Eastern Campaign

Around the time Rakkis departed Kehjistan, a cleric by the name of Akkhan forged an order known as the crusaders. He sent them on a mission to the east to seek out a means (however it manifested) to purify the Zakarum faith. The impetus for this campaign stemmed from Akkhan's belief that the church had strayed from the original teachings of Akarat.

1060 Anno Kehjistani—The Founding of Westmarch

After years of warring with the scattered tribes and civilizations of the west, Rakkis ended his journey by founding Westmarch and becoming its king. This nation was so named in honor of the general's long and arduous campaign.

1080–1100 Anno Kehjistani—
The Passing of the Horadrim

All records indicate that around this time the Horadric monastery was abandoned and left to ruin. Tristram, however, continued to prosper, although it would always remain a small settlement. Generations of townsfolk would live and die there, completely unaware of the Crimson Soulstone buried beneath them.

By 1100, the Horadrim's activities in other parts of the world had ceased. It appears that the order, with no quests left to undertake, had at last dissolved and faded into legend.

1150 Anno Kehjistani—The Zakarum Reformation

A bold new Que-Hegan, Zebulon I, initiated a sweeping reformation of the Zakarum Church. Rumor has it he did so inspired by visions from Akarat himself. Zebulon urged the faith to align with its more ascetic and humble origins. This act was well received by the people, and it sparked a surge in independent worship, secularism, and mysticism.

Note, however, that the orthodox archbishops of the Zakarum High Council viewed this turn of events as a grievous erosion of the church's power. Regardless, they were unable to stop the tide of change due to Zebulon's revered status with commoners.

1202 Anno Kehjistani—The date of Deckard Cain's birth.

1225 Anno Kehjistani— The Zakarum Inquisition

With the ascension of Que-Hegan Karamat, the Zakarum High Council fulfilled its long-sought goal to unravel Zebulon I's reformations. The archbishops manipulated the church's new leader into launching a strict system of worship that imposed harsh punishments on nonconformists. Missionary work took on increasingly martial overtones.

This, dear reader, all culminated in the heinous Zakarum Inquisition. The church purged various sects of the faith and brutally suppressed other religions, such as Skatsim.

1247 Anno Kehjistani—Order of Paladins

Unwilling to continue the inquisition's terrible methods, a group of Zakarum paladins broke away from the church. They vowed that their new Order of Paladins would protect the innocent and fight the corruption that darkened the once-brilliant heart of their religion. These rebels ventured into western lands to begin their noble campaign.

1258 Anno Kehjistani—The Crowning of King Leoric

At the behest of the Zakarum High Council, the Kehjistani lord Leoric set out to govern the land of Khanduras. This decision, it seems, was due in large part to the urgings of a powerful archbishop named Lazarus.

The ever-dutiful Leoric traveled to Khanduras and declared himself its king. He converted Tristram into the region's capital and even transformed the crumbling Horadric monastery into a glorious Zakarum cathedral.

It is vital to note that Lazarus accompanied Leoric on this journey. Upon arriving in Tristram, the archbishop secretly released Diablo from imprisonment. Indeed, it appears that this had been the archbishop's goal all along. I believe he was under Mephisto's influence before setting out for Tristram, where he then began to serve Diablo.

Once freed, Diablo subtly attempted to possess Leoric without success. I believe this occurred over a number of years, for Tristram experienced a period of peace and tranquility under its new king. Eventually, however, the Lord of Terror began stripping away at the king's sanity, sending the noble ruler into the depths of madness.

1263 Anno Kehjistani— The Darkening of Tristram

Increasingly deranged, Leoric began seeing enemies in all places, even among his friends and allies. He ordered the execution and torture of innocent townsfolk. The king also declared war on neighboring Westmarch, believing that the region was plotting against him. Along with a number of loyal followers, Leoric's eldest son, Aidan, departed for Westmarch to wage his father's ill-begotten campaign.

Lazarus secretly kidnapped Leoric's youngest son, Albrecht, and presented him before Diablo. The Lord of Terror possessed the boy, twisting the prince's body into a monstrous demonic form. Albrecht's disappearance drove Leoric into an even graver state of paranoia, and he lashed out against all those whom, in his madness, he deemed responsible for his son's mysterious fate.

Westmarch's superior armies crushed the forces of Leoric. Lachdanan, captain of the king's soldiers, returned from the disastrous conflict only to see his home in shambles. It was this brave and tragic man who finally slew Leoric, thereby putting an end to the king's reign. Thereafter Lachdanan and his comrades buried Leoric's body somewhere deep in the labyrinthine catacombs beneath Tristram.

Demons continued terrorizing the people of Tristram. All seemed lost until Aidan returned from Westmarch. Hoping to find his missing brother, the young warrior and his allies forged into the depths of the cathedral. During this harrowing journey, Aidan was forced to strike down his own father, who had been reanimated as the Skeleton King. The prince also vanquished Lazarus and a number of fetid demons. Ultimately, Aidan slew Diablo, only to find that in doing so, he had also killed Albrecht.

Nihlathak, the barbarian elder who helped
Baal bypass the guardians at Mount
Arreat's summit. In large part, it was due to
his ill-begotten actions that I was later
forced to destroy the Worldstone.

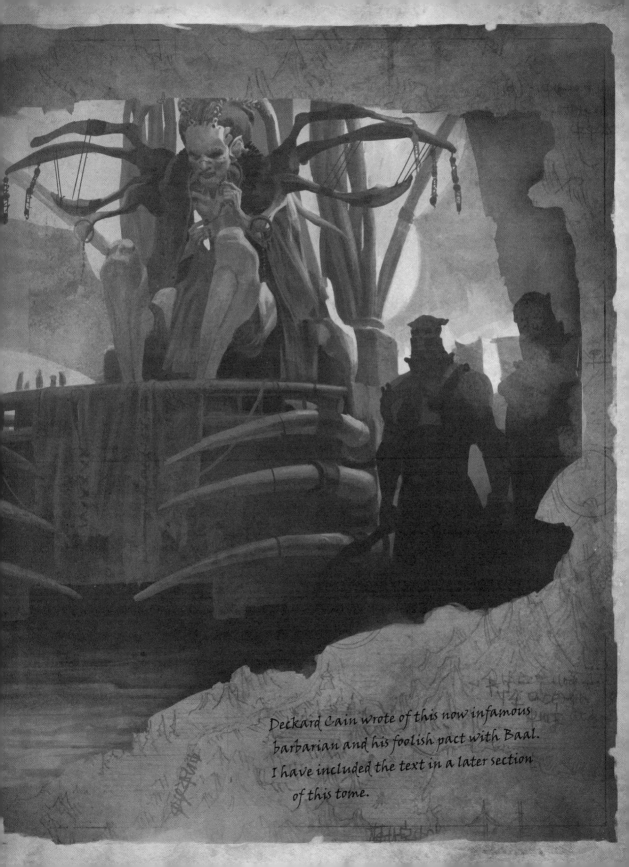

Deckard Cain wrote of this now infamous
barbarian and his foolish pact with Baal.
I have included the text in a later section
of this tome.

In the weeks that followed, Aidan became increasingly distant and withdrawn. He sought solace from only one individual in all of Tristram—the witch Adria. I later learned the cause of Aidan's troubles: in a courageous (albeit reckless) act to contain Diablo's essence, he had plunged the Crimson Soulstone into his own body.

The sad truth here is that Aidan would eventually succumb to the Lord of Terror's influence. Known henceforth as the Dark Wanderer, he departed Tristram and ventured east to liberate Baal and Mephisto. Adria left the town as well and traveled to Caldeum, where she eventually gave birth to a daughter named Leah.

As for Tristram, demons returned to the town en masse and slaughtered the inhabitants. Indeed, there was no respite or salvation for these people, only death and suffering. I survived this tragedy, though I was imprisoned by the foul minions of the Burning Hells.

1264 Anno Kehjistani— The Dark Wanderer

Archangel Tyrael learned of the Dark Wanderer and his plans. The Aspect of Justice confronted him in the tomb of Tal Rasha, but the archangel was overcome by the combined might of the Wanderer and the newly liberated Baal. The two Prime Evils imprisoned Tyrael in the ancient tomb.

It was around this time that a band of heroes rescued me from Tristram. I helped them as best I could. Together we freed the rogue monastery of Eastgate Keep from demonic influence and then followed the Wanderer's path to the tomb of Tal Rasha. There, we released Tyrael from his bonds and swiftly continued our journey.

It is important to note here that during this time, my companions faced and defeated Andariel and Duriel, for it appears that these Lesser Evils had decided to aid Diablo.

The Dark Wanderer eluded us at every step. He managed to free Mephisto within Travincal. It was then that the last vestiges of Aidan disappeared and Diablo took on a more fitting demonic form. He ventured into the Hells to muster his followers, while Baal set out to Mount Arreat, home of the Worldstone. Mephisto remained in Travincal to continue asserting his influence over the Zakarum Church and its crazed followers.

I cannot overstate the momentous events that followed.

Against all odds, my companions defeated both Mephisto and Diablo (the latter within the very depths of the Burning Hells) and captured them within their respective soulstones. The heroes went on to sunder the crystals in the blistering Hellforge, thereby casting Mephisto's and Diablo's essences into what I speculate to be an otherworldly realm called the Abyss.

In the wake of this victory, my companions fixed their gaze on Baal. The Lord of Destruction had begun rampaging toward the sacred summit of Mount Arreat. You must understand that from the moment of Sanctuary's creation, this mountain had acted as a protective shell around the Worldstone. It was this—the Heart of Creation itself—that Baal planned to find and corrupt.

1265 Anno Kehjistani— The Lord of Destruction

Atop Arreat, my companions defeated Baal, but not before the demon had tainted the Worldstone with evil. Dear reader, understand that by doing so, the Lord of Destruction had damned humanity to darkness. Our fall to evil appeared inevitable.

Only Tyrael knew of our terrible fate. Steeling himself, he cast his angelic blade, El'druin, into the Worldstone. The resulting explosion shattered the crystal and leveled Mount Arreat. I have come to believe even Tyrael was destroyed in the process.

But it must be stated that this act, however catastrophic it was, thwarted Baal's designs for humanity.

This is true. It would take many years for my essence to rematerialize, thus allowing me to return to the High Heavens.

1265 Anno Kehjistani — Caldeum Ascendant

Once it was revealed that demons controlled the Zakarum Church, public opinion of the organization plummeted. Indeed, Kurast and Travincal had suffered greatly with the Dark Wanderer's arrival in the city and the events that followed.

After a series of deft political maneuvers, Emperor Hakan I moved the capital of Kehjistan to Caldeum and secured power there. It should be stated that this was no easy feat. Powerful trade groups controlled much of Caldeum, and the emperor's reputation had suffered in the wake of Zakarum corruption. But Hakan was a brilliant diplomat, and he used his talents to forge alliances and gain the respect of the city's nobility.

In the years that followed, Caldeum also proved to be a sanctuary for the remaining members of the Zakarum Church. These individuals flooded into the city to begin their lives anew. It was at this time that Caldeum, which had always been an important city, became perhaps the most powerful and influential urban center in all of Sanctuary.

During this time, in the year 1272, Deckard Cain traveled to Caldeum and took Leah into his care.

1272 Anno Kehjistani — The First Ones

Long before I encountered them, a group of young scholars discovered a hidden archive of Horadric texts in the city of Gea Kul. They brought these lost tomes before the famed litterateur Garreth Rau, who was so amazed by the find that he took lead of the scholars and set out to reforge the Horadrim. The members of this fledgling order became known as the First Ones. There was, however, a darker truth to Rau and his seemingly noble plans: he was beholden to the will of Belial, the Lord of Lies. Gradually, this man used his influence and power to transform Gea Kul into a warren of torture and hopelessness.

With young Leah at my side, I uncovered Rau's ultimate goal while investigating rumors of the re-formed Horadrim. He planned to resurrect an army of fallen sorcerers entombed beneath Gea Kul — victims of a horrific battle waged during the Mage Clan Wars. Alongside the brave uncorrupted members of the First Ones and Mikulov, a monk from the kingdom of Ivgorod, Leah and I helped bring Rau's schemes to an end.

With the passing of Deckard Cain, I have continued his work. Soon this task will fall to you, Horadrim.

Over these twenty years, Cain dedicated his life to investigating the End of Days.

1285 Anno Kehjistani—The Prime Evil

After the fall of the Prime Evils, Belial and Azmodan plotted an invasion of Sanctuary. I broached this subject with the Angiris Council, but they did not heed my warnings. Therefore, I made my decision to join the ranks of mankind as a mortal.

When I fell to Sanctuary, my dissipating angelic powers roused the dead outside New Tristram, a settlement built near the remains of the old town. The ordeal left me powerless to help the townsfolk defend their homes. No, salvation came from a different source: a brave mortal whose nephalem powers had awakened. Sadly, Cain fell during these events. His loss will be felt for many years to come.

Together with Leah, the nephalem, and other valorous mortals, I set out to Caldeum, where Belial had assumed the guise of a new emperor, Hakan II. Leah's estranged mother, the witch Adria, soon joined us. Her guidance led us to the Black Soulstone, an incredible artifact that contained the essences of five of the seven Lords of the Hells. After capturing Belial and Azmodan, Adria had us believe that she would destroy the crystal, thus banishing evil from existence once and for all.

The valiant nephalem defeated Belial in Caldeum, and the Lord of Lies was drawn into the recesses of the Black Soulstone. My companions and I then set out for Arreat Crater, where Azmodan had unleashed the legions of Hell upon the mortal world.

Many lives were lost. Many horrors were faced. While other mortals cowered, the nephalem forged onward, striking down Azmodan. As with Belial, the last demon lord was contained within the Black Soulstone. A glorious victory lay ahead. . . . And that was when Adria unveiled her true allegiance.

For at least twenty years, she had served Diablo. She had conceived Leah, whose father was the Dark Wanderer, for the sole purpose of acting as a vessel for the Lord of Terror. Diablo consumed the essences of the other Lords of the Hells trapped within the Black Soulstone, thus becoming the Prime Evil. Possessing Leah's body, the terrible entity stormed the High Heavens and laid waste to the angelic realm.

Atop the great Crystal Arch, the nephalem finally vanquished the Prime Evil and cast the entity from the Heavens. The Black Soulstone, however, escaped destruction. Still roiling with the Prime Evil's essence, it was placed in the care of the Angiris Council.

This act marked the beginning of a new era in the history of angels and mortals alike. But whether or not Diablo's reign of terror had truly come to an end remained unclear.

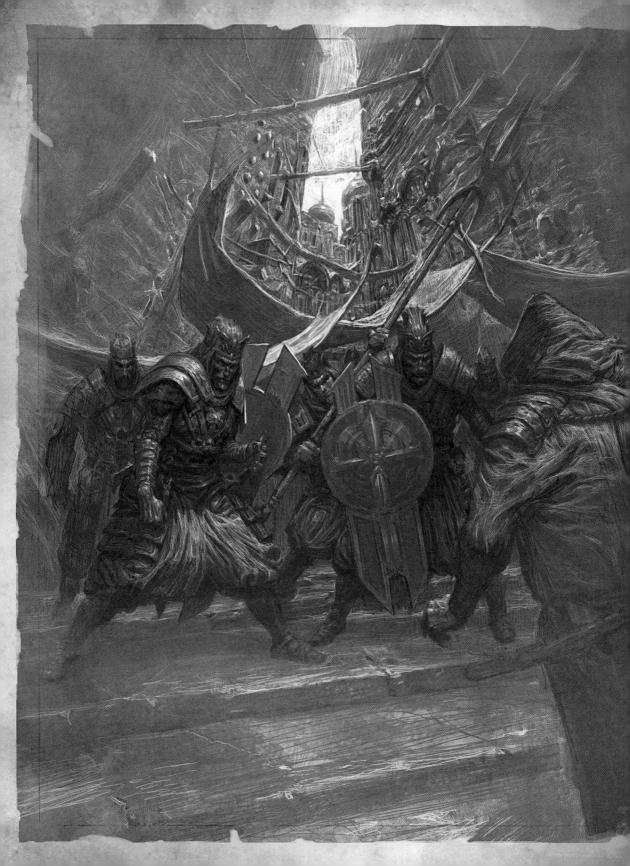

Factions of Sanctuary

Amazons

* Leader: *Queen Xaera*
* Base of Operations: *Temis, Skovos Isles*
* Standing: *Active*
* Number of Members: *Est. 5,000 (fully trained soldiers of the amazon caste)*

The amazons are an elite martial caste of the Askari culture. Tales of their almost preternatural skill with bows, javelins, and spears are well-known throughout Sanctuary. The highly trained members of this caste fulfill a range of duties, from defending the borders of their sun-drenched homeland, the Skovos Isles, to guarding the vast Askari merchant fleets that sail to the far corners of the world.

It should be noted here that the amazons are not merely soldiers. They are bound to the matriarchal Askari government. Two queens reign over the Skovos Isles, one of whom heads the amazons. The other monarch rules a caste of mystics and spiritual leaders known as the oracles. This has been the way of things since ancient times.

Assassins

* Leader: *Unknown*
* Base of Operations: *Unknown*
* Standing: *Active*
* Number of Members: *Unknown*

Mystery shrouds the assassins (also known as the Viz-Jaq'taar or the Order of the Mage Slayers). The very name of their order is whispered in hushed and fearful tones by those who practice magic. I have met a few of these assassins, but the truth is that I still know very little concerning the group's rites, numbers, and leadership. What I am aware of, however, is this: after the disastrous Mage Clan Wars, the Vizjerei leaders created the Viz-Jaq'taar to watch over all sorcerers and hunt down any foolish enough to delve into demonology or other outlawed practices. To avoid the potentially corruptive influence of magic, assassins were strictly forbidden from directly wielding arcane energies. Instead, the members were instructed to hone their bodies into weapons and employ ingenious devices and enchanted traps to match the powers of their sorcerous enemies.

Barbarian Tribes

* Leader: *Varied (individual chiefs lead each tribe)*
* Base of Operations: *Mount Arreat (formerly)*
* Standing: *Active*
* Number of Tribes: *Est. 32 (formerly)*

Once, there were numerous barbarian tribes, many of which had existed since before recorded history. Each one traced its lineage back to the mighty nephalem Bul-Kathos. Each one sang epic sagas of its own great warrior ancestors. For millennia, these proud and indomitable tribes lived around Mount Arreat, a place considered sacred to the barbarian people. Indeed, despite whatever blood feuds or rivalries existed among the groups, they were all devoted to protecting the mountain.

In the year 1265, tragedy befell the mighty barbarians. Arreat was torn asunder in a catastrophic explosion, wiping entire tribes from existence. Ever since that apocalyptic day, few barbarian enclaves have remained at the smoldering corpse of the mountain. Most have disbanded entirely, their members scattered like leaves in the wind. It is said they search the world for a new purpose—a new vigil—to give their lives meaning.

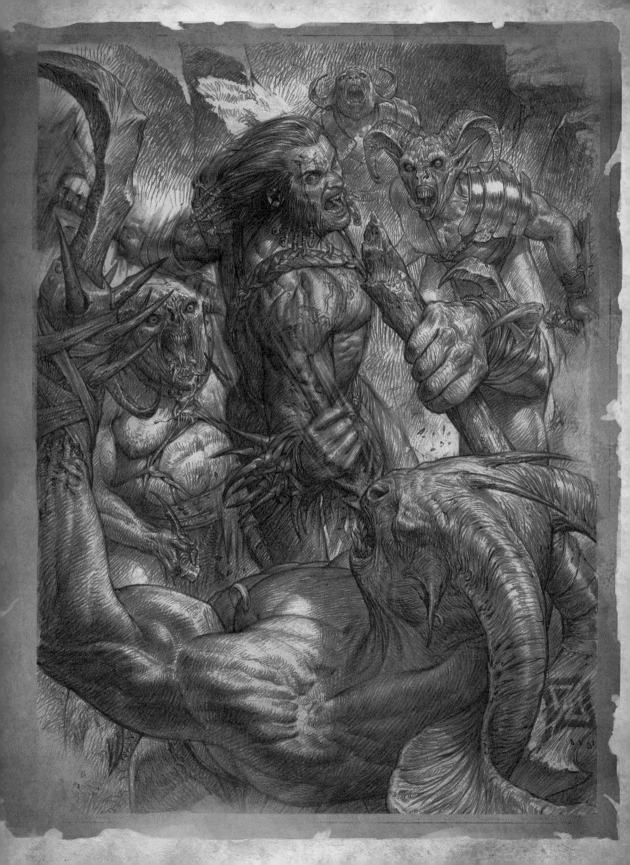

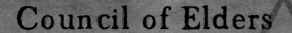

Council of Elders

* Leader: *Shared among council members*
* Base of Operations: *Harrogath*
* Standing: *Inactive*
* Number of Members: *13*

The Council of Elders (sometimes called the Elders of Harrogath) was an order of venerated and sage barbarians. From passages I have found in the ancient *Scéal Fada* tome, it appears this group came into being in the early days of the barbarian civilization. Over the generations, the council provided guidance to the myriad tribes that lived in Mount Arreat's shadow. When Baal launched his assault against the barbarians in 1265, nearly all the Elders sacrificed themselves to cast a protective barrier around the bastion of Harrogath. To fully appreciate the council's act, you must understand that Harrogath was Arreat's last defense—the only place that stood between the Lord of Destruction and the mountain's sacred summit.

Only one Elder did not take part in this selfless act. His name was Nihlathak, and I have written of him elsewhere. Suffice it to say, Baal's invasion brought an end to the Council of Elders. Now that the barbarian tribes are in disarray, I do not know when or if the order will return.

The Coven

* Leader: *Maghda*
* Base of Operations: *Unknown*
* Standing: *Active*
* Number of Members: *Est. 500*

Mark the Coven well, for it represents one of the greatest threats to our world. I believe this depraved group to be an offshoot of the ancient Triune. There are, however, some notable differences between the two. Unlike the old Triune, the Coven makes no attempt to hide its association with demons, its merciless torture methods, or its grotesque rituals. Secondly, I have suspicions that the Coven serves the Lesser Evils Azmodan and Belial, whereas the ancient Triune bowed to the will of the Prime Evils.

This is merely speculation on my part, but I feel it is important to write here. After all, the Lesser Evils very likely have sinister designs for our world, plans that may soon unfold. As such, we should watch the Coven's activities with utmost scrutiny.

Based on my recent experiences battling the Coven, I believe its membership far exceeded Cain's estimate.

Crusaders

* Leader: *Akkhan (formerly); currently no centralized leadership*
* Base of Operations: *None*
* Standing: *Active*
* Number of Members: *Est. 300-400*

The crusader order arose in the eleventh century Anno Kehjistani, a time when the world was undergoing fundamental changes. The Zakarum Church had become the dominant religion in Kehjistan. Rakkis had set off on his grand campaign to the west. Amid these earth-shaking events, the Zakarum cleric Akkhan began noticing subtle signs that darkness was eating away at the heart of his religion. He formed the order in reaction to this burgeoning corruption. The crusaders, holy warriors of incredible martial prowess and determination, traveled east to search for a means to purify the Zakarum faith. Over two centuries later, this organization still exists, its adherents unwavering in their desire to fulfill Akkhan's charge.

One subject I feel it prudent to elaborate on here is why the order traveled east specifically. I myself believe that the crusaders' destination was tied to the life of Akarat, founder of the Zakarum faith. Some of the church's more apocryphal writings (such as the scrolls of Sarjuq) say that he was last seen wandering into the eastern lands beyond Kehjistan's borders. I have no doubt Akkhan was aware of these stories. Perhaps he sent his followers to that corner of the world in the hopes they would find some as yet undiscovered writings or relics left behind by Akarat. This is mere speculation on my part, but I find it an adequate explanation for the course taken by the crusaders.

See Deckard Cain's more intricate account of this order, which I have included in the 'Fate of the Black Soulstone' section.

Druids

* Leader: *Greenwalker Ciódan*
* Base of Operations: *Túr Dúlra, Scosglen*
* Standing: *Active*
* Number of Members: *Unknown*
(although I estimate that at least 500 high-ranking warriors watch over and guide much of druidic culture)

The druids are a most intriguing order, a collective of warrior-poets who inhabit the verdant forests of Scosglen. They live by the *Caoi Dúlra*, a philosophy passed down by the nephalem Vasily that exhorts oneness with the natural world. The druids are so tied to the land that they can commune with animals and even plants, calling on their aid in battle. I have witnessed these feats firsthand and know them to be more than legend.

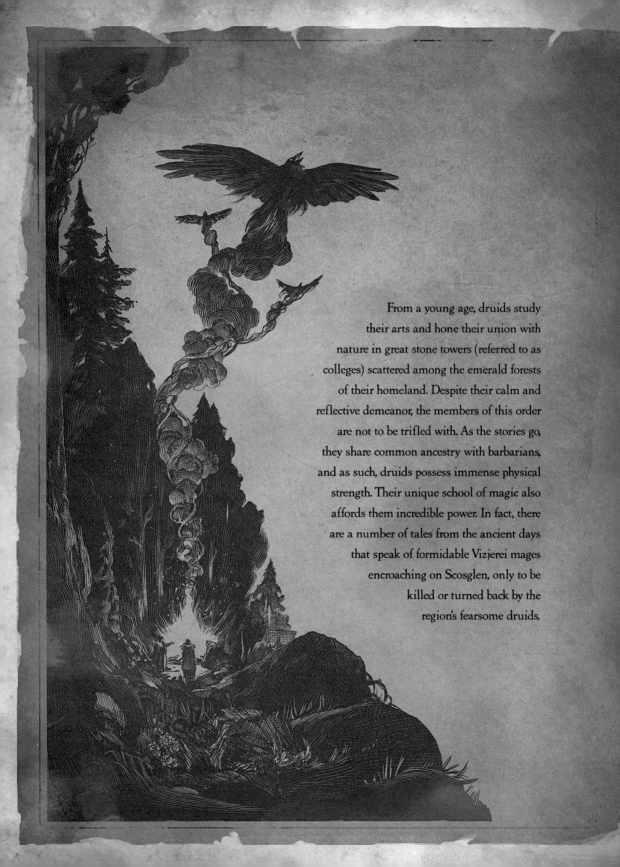

From a young age, druids study
their arts and hone their union with
nature in great stone towers (referred to as
colleges) scattered among the emerald forests
of their homeland. Despite their calm and
reflective demeanor, the members of this order
are not to be trifled with. As the stories go,
they share common ancestry with barbarians,
and as such, druids possess immense physical
strength. Their unique school of magic also
affords them incredible power. In fact, there
are a number of tales from the ancient days
that speak of formidable Vizjerei mages
encroaching on Scosglen, only to be
killed or turned back by the
region's fearsome druids.

The Edyrem

* Leader: *Uldyssian ul-Diomed (formerly)*
* Base of Operations: *Kehjan and surrounding regions (formerly)*
* Standing: *Inactive*
* Number of Members: *Est. 3,000 (formerly)*

The edyrem, or "those who have seen," were an order of mortals whose nephalem powers flourished during the Sin War. Due to a lack of records, it is impossible for us to know precisely what kinds of abilities these individuals wielded. It is safe to assume, however, that they would have surpassed even the greatest mages of that era.

The edyrem waged war against the Temple of the Triune and the Cathedral of Light, fearing that the influence of the two religions would destroy humanity. After the Sin War, the edyrem's powers were leeched away, and their memories were expunged. It is difficult to imagine these individuals returning to their mundane lives as farmers and tradesmen after they had attained such incredible heights of human potential.

Horadrim

* Leader: *Tal Rasha (formerly), Jered Cain (formerly),*
  Garreth Rau (formerly), Thomas and Cullen
* Base of Operations: *Gea Kul*
* Standing: *Active*
* Number of Members: *Est. 7-12 (formerly, original core members),*
  now 10 (I base this current number on my last communication
  with Thomas and Cullen.)

Nearly three centuries ago, Archangel Tyrael forged the Horadrim, a band of preeminent mages that set out to imprison the three Prime Evils: Diablo, Mephisto, and Baal. The order succeeded in its grave and perilous task, but not without many sacrifices. Indeed, the mages were forever changed by the horrors they faced.

The ranks of the Horadrim now far outnumber this old estimate.

Nonetheless they continued their work, documenting everything they knew or could learn about the forces of the Burning Hells and the High Heavens. In the decades following the defeat of the Prime Evils, the Horadrim gradually faded away, leaving only their great legacy behind.

It was this legacy that I inherited generations later. As a caretaker of Horadric knowledge and a direct descendant of Jered Cain, I considered myself the sole living member of the organization. My thinking on this changed when I discovered that a group of scholars in the city of Gea Kul had banded together to carry on the Horadric teachings. These individuals have dedicated themselves to the order, and I believe that in the years to come they will accomplish feats worthy of the original Horadrim.

Deckard wrote more about the Horadrim in the Book of Cain. I have compiled information concerning the newest incarnation of the order earlier in this tome.

The Iron Wolves

* Leader: *Commander Asheara*
* Base of Operations: *Caldeum*
* Standing: *Active*
* Number of Members: *Est. 550*

Mercenary companies are notorious for their habit of shifting allegiances, but the Iron Wolves are somewhat different. Although bold and reckless, they value loyalty and duty above all else. Their members are hardened veterans who excel in disciplines ranging from swordsmanship to the arcane sciences.

After the fall of Kurast, the Zakarum Church hired the Iron Wolves to retrieve Kehjistan's new ruler, Hakan II, from his home in the northern reaches of Sanctuary. With the task complete, the Iron Wolves became the child emperor's personal guards. This single event has elevated the mercenary company to a level of power and influence hitherto unheard of for an organization of its kind.

When corruption seeped throughout Caldeum, Emperor Hakan II replaced the Iron Wolves with his personal Imperial Guard. Asheara and her loyal soldiers nonetheless aided us in saving the city.

Mage Clans

• Leader: *Master Valthek*
• Base of Operations: *Yshari Sanctum, Caldeum*
• Standing: *Active*
• Number of Members: *Est. 500*
(excluding those not affiliated with the Yshari Sanctum)

Of the myriad factions and orders in existence, I believe it is the mage clans that have shaped mortal destiny the most. As I have written extensively on the history of these enclaves in other tomes, I will focus here on the status of the clans in the modern era.

Five in particular remain notable: the Ennead, Ammuit, Vizjerei, Taan, and Zann Esu. For centuries following the Mage Clan Wars, the populations of these once-influential groups dwindled. This trend saw a reversal in recent years due to the acts of Caldeum's Trade Consortium. In seeking to make their city a beacon of learning, the mercantile rulers worked to unite the mage clans and build the great Yshari Sanctum. This wondrous academy, filled with a treasure trove of arcana, has become a place of learning and growth for the various clans. I believe that the Sanctum stands as the greatest symbol of mage power and unity since the golden age of magic.

Necromancers

* Leader: *Deathspeaker Jurdann*
* Base of Operations: *Eastern Kehjistan*
* Standing: *Active*
* Number of Members: *Est. 150*

The necromancers, or priests of Rathma, are a misunderstood order, feared by many for their ability to interact with the dead. It was the legendary nephalem Rathma who taught mortals this art of bending the line between life and death. According to the *Books of Kalan*, the patron of the necromancers also bestowed on his followers a most vital task: to preserve the Balance between light and dark, thereby preventing both angels and demons from holding too much sway over humanity. It is interesting to note that the first necromancers may have arisen during the Sin War, a time when the mortal world was under grave threat from the High Heavens and the Burning Hells.

As to the inner workings of the order, I know very little. The priests of Rathma live in a vast subterranean city somewhere in Kehjistan's eastern jungles. This isolation has spared them from the influence of other mage clans, allowing the necromancers to develop wholly unique rites and arcane sciences. I briefly traveled with a necromancer in the past. Through that experience I have come to believe that the priests of Rathma can be powerful and trustworthy allies to have at one's side in these uncertain times.

Paladins

* Leader: *Grand Marshal Elyas (formerly)*
* Base of Operations: *Westmarch*
* Standing: *Inactive*
* Number of Members: *Est. 250 (formerly)*

Paladins are members of a martial wing of the Zakarum faith, holy warriors trained to wield the powers of the Light in battle. Of these righteous individuals, I wish to write of a specific group known as the Order of Paladins. During the dark years of the Zakarum Inquisition (a subject which I elaborate on elsewhere), an enclave of paladins splintered away from the church. They vehemently condemned the methods of the inquisition, vowing that they would no longer continue the legacy of bloodshed. Pledging to protect the innocent from all forms of evil, the valiant renegades journeyed to Westmarch, where they were embraced by King Cornelius. In recent years, this order has merged with the Knights of Westmarch, a group of paladins that had already existed in the kingdom.

Patriarchs

* Leader: *Shared among the Patriarchs*
* Base of Operations: *Ivgorod*
* Standing: *Active*
* Number of Members: *9*

Maintaining balance between the forces of order and chaos is ingrained in Ivgorod's ancient culture and beliefs. The kingdom's supreme governmental and religious rulers, the Patriarchs, are a reflection of this. In total, nine leaders exist. Four are pledged to order; four are pledged to chaos; and one remains neutral. Ivgorod's religion—known as Sahptev—venerates one thousand and one gods, and it is said that the Patriarchs speak for these deities. As such, their will goes unquestioned by every man, woman, and child of the nation.

Regarding the origins of the Patriarchs, ancient Sahptev scrolls claim that long ago the thousand and one gods chose nine humans to found and rule over what would become Ivgorod. The Patriarchs are believed to be the reincarnations of those nine founders.

Rogues

* Leader: *High Priestess Akara*
* Base of Operations: *Eastgate Keep, Khanduras*
* Standing: *Active*
* Number of Members: *Est. 40*

Rogues are members of a secretive guild calling itself the Sisters of the Sightless Eye. Among other things, they are renowned for their unmatched skill with the bow and arrow. With this in mind, it may come as no surprise that the rogue order was founded by amazons from the Skovos Isles, who are also famed for their adept use of ranged weaponry. Years ago, a group of these warrior women splintered away from Askari society, taking with them a wondrous artifact called the Sightless Eye. Legends hold that this device is a most incredible artifact. According to some accounts, the Sightless Eye grants one the ability to perceive details concerning future events. Other stories relate that the relic allows for communication between individuals across vast distances.

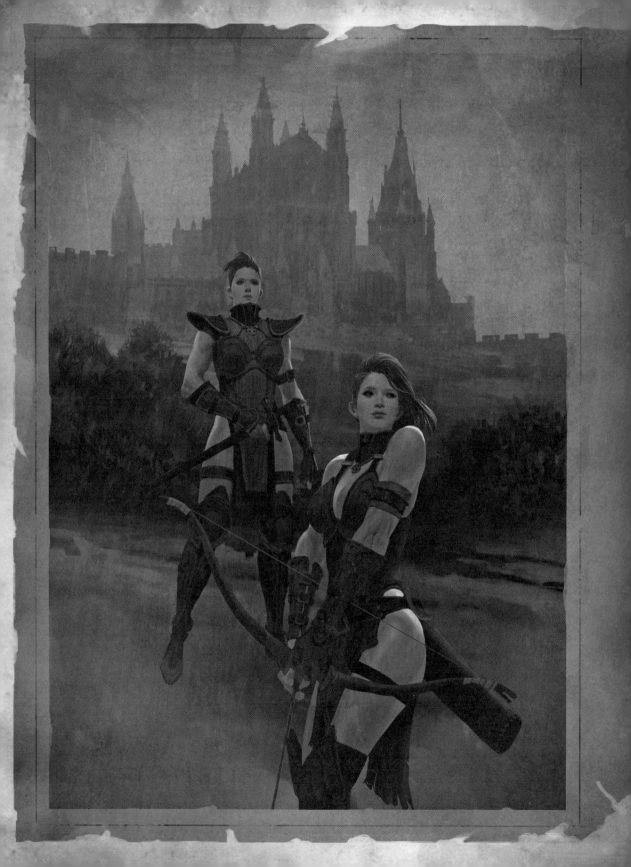

The Sisters of the Sightless Eye eventually settled in Eastgate Keep, which had fallen into abandonment after Rakkis founded the nation of Westmarch. There, they continued their own unique style of martial training, focusing on bows. It is said that the sisters recruited women from any walk of life who sought refuge in the mountain fortress and a means to forge a new destiny for themselves. Around twenty years ago, the Lesser Evil Andariel exerted her influence over the sisters, nearly breaking the order. They recovered from this tragic event, and the keep's training grounds now hum once again with the sound of bowstrings and battle cries. I should note, however, that the fate of the Sightless Eye itself remains unknown.

Skatsim

* Leader: *No centralized leadership*
* Base of Operations: *Kehjistan*
* Standing: *Active*
* Number of Members: *Est. 10,000*

I rely on the *Black Book of Lam Esen* for much of my information about Skatsim. Prior to the rise of the Zakarum Church, it was one of the most widely practiced religions in Kehjistan. At its core, Skatsim is a unique blend of faith and mysticism. Practitioners perform certain rites to attain states of clairvoyance or to perceive past and future events. The followers of Skatsim strive for a higher sense of being—a transcendence of self. Although the popularity of this faith has waned over the centuries, its influence can be seen in the Taan mage clan, which shares many of the old religion's practices.

It appears this speculation is grounded in fact. One of my comrades, a member of the templar named Kormac, learned of his order's heinous practices.

Templar

* Leader: *Unknown (although I have heard references to the leader being called the "grand maester")*
* Base of Operations: *Westmarch*
* Standing: *Active*
* Number of Members: *Unknown*

The templar order of Westmarch is something of an enigma to me. Some stories depict the organization's members as former criminals who have been given a chance to atone for their sins and walk the path of righteousness. Other, more unsettling accounts paint the templar in a much different light. If these rumors are to be believed, the order abducts innocent citizens and subjects them to horrific torture, purging their memories and molding them into zealous adherents. I cannot corroborate any of these darker tales with facts, but the mere existence of them makes me fearful of the group's true intentions.

The Temple of the Triune

* Leader: *Lucion, the Primus (formerly)*
* Base of Operations: *Kehjan (formerly)*
* Standing: *Active*
* Number of Members: *Unknown (In ancient times,*
I believe the temple's followers would have numbered in the tens of thousands.)

Nearly three millennia ago, the Temple of the Triune (or Cult of the Three) arose in the sprawling empire of Kehjan. It was forged by none other than the Prime Evils of the Burning Hells as a means to influence the hearts of mankind. The cult revolved around the worship of three benevolent deities—Dialon, the spirit of Determination (represented by a ram), Bala, the spirit of Creation (represented by a leaf), and Mefis, the spirit of Love (represented by a red circle)—who were in reality Diablo, Baal, and Mephisto. It is said that the number three was used symbolically in the cult's architecture and methods of operation. One need only look to the Triune's military wing, the Peace Warders, for examples. They traveled in threes at all times, each member serving one of the cult's seemingly compassionate deities.

At the apex of its power, the Triune fell to Uldyssian ul-Diomed and his fellow awakened nephalem, the edyrem. It is clear, however, that remnants of the cult persisted long after this point. Confined to the shadows, they eschewed the Triune's benevolent façade and preserved its vile secrets, faithfully awaiting a sign from the Prime Evils. I believe that the latest incarnation of the Triune is a group calling itself the Coven (of which I wrote on earlier). Whether or not other splinter groups of the cult still exist is a mystery, but I should think they do. After all, the influence of the Prime Evils is not so easily purged from the world of mortals.

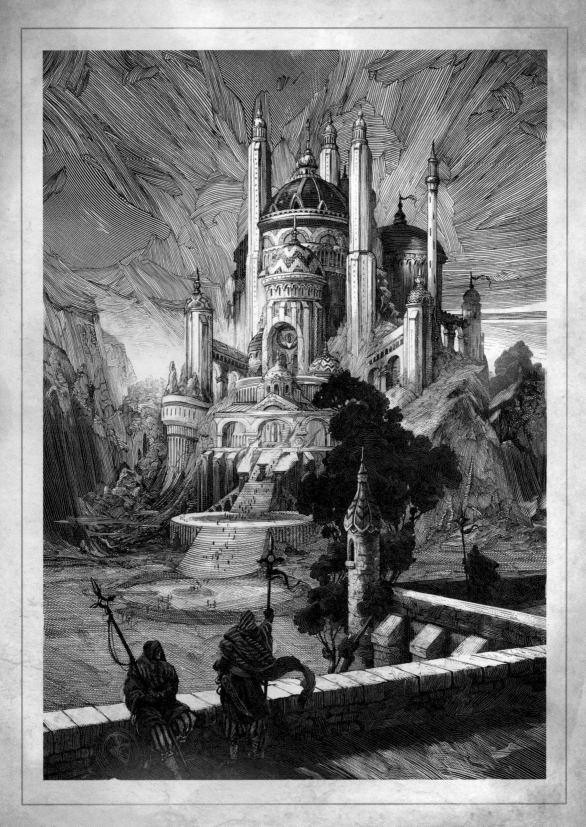

The Thieves Guild

* Leader: *Unknown (As with the assassins, the guild strives to mask its leadership.)*
* Base of Operations: *Westmarch and other regions of the west*
* Standing: *Active*
* Number of Members: *Est. 300 (including all ranks)*

The Thieves Guild arose in the years after Rakkis founded the nation of Westmarch. Since that time, the criminal network has spread to cities throughout the kingdom and beyond, delving into extortion, bribery, smuggling, murder, and all manner of illicit activities.

The Thieves Guild goes to great lengths to keep its inner workings a mystery to outsiders. However, I have come to learn that the order usually recruits its members from the poverty-stricken slums. These initiates train in pickpocketing, and those who show promise ascend in rank, much as a craftsman would in a legitimate trade guild. It should be noted that climbing the ladder of the guild's hierarchy grants one increasingly lucrative—and dangerous—work.

Trade Consortium

* Leader: *Trade Consortium Council*
* Base of Operations: *Caldeum*
* Standing: *Active*
* Number of Members: *Est. 10,000 (including common merchants)*

Many mercantile guilds exist throughout Sanctuary, but one—Caldeum's Trade Consortium— is of particular interest to me. Through war, through famine, and through the passing of empires, this order has endured and flourished. I believe part of the consortium's strength comes from its inclusionary methods. The order's leaders do not fight the winds of change; they embrace them. This is evidenced by their decision to allow the great Zakarum cathedral Saldencal to be built within Caldeum. Later, the consortium constructed the Yshari Sanctum, a center of arcane studies. These two acts alone have won the consortium many allies among the Zakarum faithful and mage clans. More recently, Kehjistan's late emperor Hakan I declared Caldeum his seat of power. Rather than resist this sudden turn of events, the consortium deftly maneuvered through the mire of politics and managed to retain its influential status in the city.

Zakarum

* Leader: *Que-Hegan Dirae*
* Base of Operations: *Saldencal, Caldeum*
* Standing: *Active*
* Number of Members: *Est. 50,000*

Who, living today, does not know of the Zakarum faith? Who has not seen its loyalists preaching of the inner Light or of the founder, Akarat, from the cobblestone streets of Westmarch to the winding bazaars of Caldeum? Dear reader, in the last few centuries, this organization has impacted the world in fundamental and far-reaching ways. This is remarkable because the order began as nothing more than a humble group of ascetics. In time, these believers garnered the power to forge nations and raise emperors to the throne.

Recently, the Zakarum Church has lost much of its influence. The discovery that Mephisto, the Lord of Hatred, had corrupted the highest echelons of the faith—the Que-Hegan and High Council— nearly destroyed the organization. The church has since moved from Kurast to Caldeum. Under the leadership of a new Que-Hegan named Dirae, the Zakarum faithful are nursing their wounds and mending their reputation.

In closing, I should note that the Zakarum faith in Westmarch has distanced itself from the church in Kehjistan (especially after the revelation concerning Mephisto). Indeed, the western kingdom has become increasingly secular in recent years, but groups influenced by the Zakarum faith, such as the Knights of Westmarch, still exist.

Hand of Zakarum

I consider the years of the Zakarum Inquisition to be one of the darkest periods of history. Initiated by the church, this brutal campaign of conversion spread paranoia and fear throughout the lands of Kehjistan. Nonbelievers were judged as corrupt and subjected to horrific interrogations and "purification" techniques. A group of paladins known as the Hand of Zakarum acted as the vanguard of this heinous crusade. Although some of these holy warriors would later break away from the church, many more propagated the horror of the inquisition until the movement finally faded away.

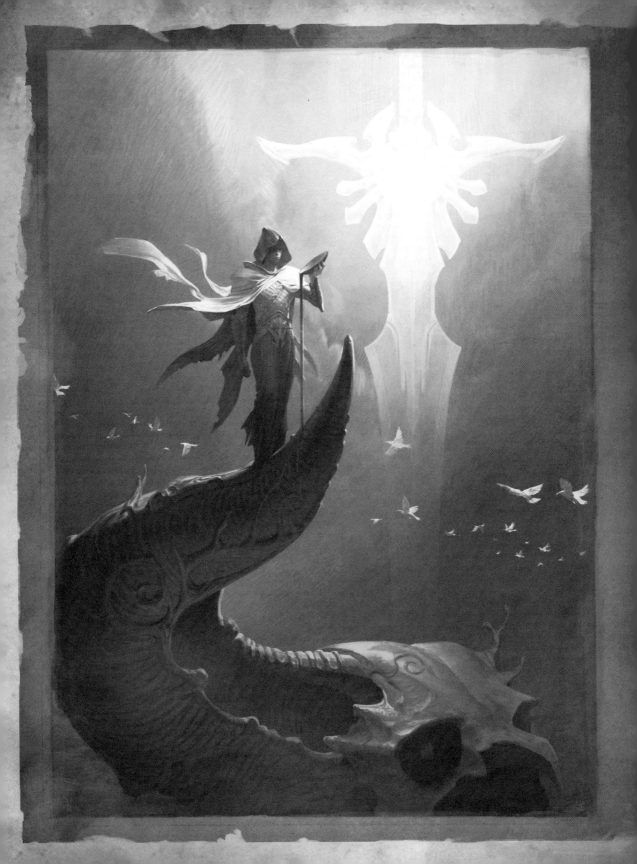

Figures of Interest

Abd al-Hazir

Abd al-Hazir is a historian and seeker of knowledge. He is considered by many to be one of the preeminent scholars of Caldeum, and for a number of years he taught in the city's most renowned academies. This rise to fame is quite impressive considering that the man was born into abject poverty. I heard that recently, Abd set off to journey the world and document its myriad peoples, creatures, and lands.

Akara

Akara is the spiritual leader of the Sisters of the Sightless Eye, a soft-spoken, inscrutable, and wise woman. I believe she is practiced in the secret and closely guarded ways of using the Sightless Eye, an incredible artifact from the Skovos Isles.

Akarat (deceased)

Countless legends exist concerning Akarat, founder of the Zakarum faith. The simple truth, however, is that his origins and life are a mystery. Even the circumstances of his death are shrouded in hearsay. It is said that after he spread his teachings in Kehjistan, he disappeared into the east and was never seen again.

Alaric (deceased)

According to the *Books of Kalan*, Alaric was from one of the first nephalem generations. He and his companions lived in what was once a grand temple in Khanduras (the ruins of this place, known as the Drowned Temple, exist to this day). After the Worldstone was altered and the nephalem powers dwindled, Alaric and his companions were beset by a cunning and duplicitous demon named Nereza. I am not fully aware of the circumstances or outcome of this conflict, but there are legends that the ghosts of Alaric and his allies still roam the shattered halls of the Drowned Temple.

Jacob Staalek, a mortal of incredible resolve and virtue. Deckard Cain detailed his life later in this section.

Ardleon

Ardleon ranks among Archangel Tyrael's boldest followers. During one of the many battles of the Eternal Conflict, this indomitable angel forged into a sea of demons before finding himself lost behind enemy lines. He only narrowly escaped death at the hands of his foes when Tyrael intervened to save him. Side by side, the two angels cut through the seething ranks of the Burning Hells to reach the Heavenly Host.

Asheara

Asheara spent many years as a member of various unscrupulous mercenary outfits. Despising the brutal tactics employed by these groups, she eventually forged the Iron Wolves, an order of sellswords that holds honor and duty above all else. I know Asheara to be strict with her followers, but also evenhanded.

Astrogha

The cunning demon Astrogha is one of Diablo's most loyal minions. From my investigations, it appears this venomous multi-legged fiend has been summoned to the mortal realm at least twice: first by the Triune during the Sin War; second by a necromancer named Karybdus in the modern era. As to Astrogha's current fate, I have heard accounts that the vile creature was banished into the depths of a mysterious artifact known as the Moon of the Spider.

Bartuc (deceased)

It is difficult to believe the stories of Bartuc, the Warlord of Blood . . . difficult to believe how a man could lose himself in such a deep abyss of depravity and barbarism. The histories state he was a Vizjerei mage practiced in the dark arts of summoning demons and unleashing them in battle. Indeed, he relished in embracing the powers of the Burning Hells without thought for the consequences.

Bartuc became infamous for his gruesome ritual of bathing in the blood of his enemies. If the Vizjerei accounts are true, this act infused the mage with incredible powers. It is even said his armor drank deep of the spilled blood, attaining a malevolent sentience of its own.

The Warlord of Blood's hubris and lust for genocide drove him to wage a terrible civil war against his own Vizjerei clan. His bloody rampage was ultimately put to an end when he was slain by his brother, the mage Horazon.

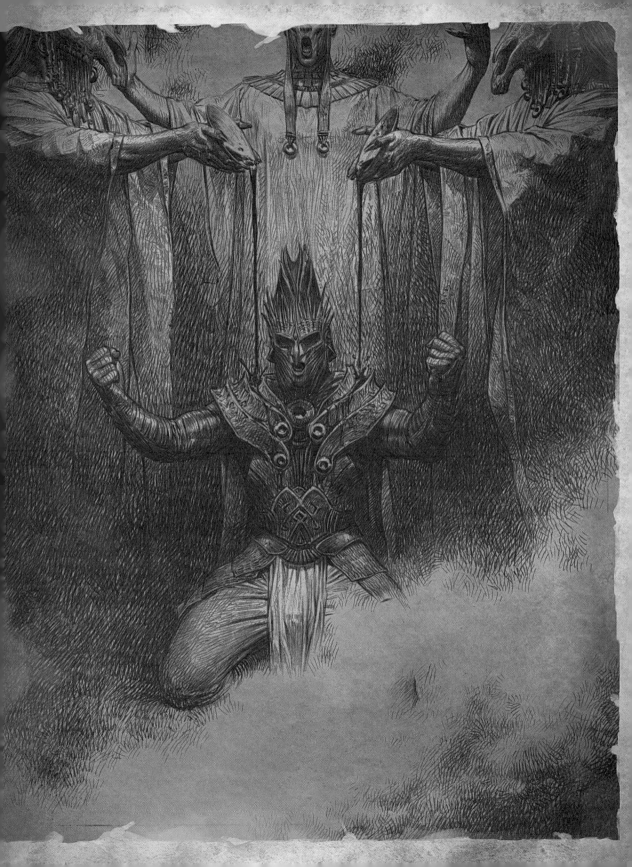

Benu (deceased)

I find the beliefs and ways of the umbaru people who inhabit the Teganze jungle endlessly intriguing. One recent story recounted to me concerning this culture's spiritual warriors, the witch doctors, is about an individual named Benu. It is said this young man bravely sacrificed himself to slay a demon of anguish that had assumed the guise of a fellow umbaru. Some witch doctors claim that ever since this event, the spirit of Benu has whispered to them from beyond the grave, passing on sage wisdom and guidance.

Charsi

When she was very young, the barbarian Charsi and her parents were ambushed by a throng of murderous khazra. The mother and father managed to hide their child away in the surrounding wilds before the goatmen ruthlessly slaughtered them. Quite by chance, members of the Sisters of the Sightless Eye later found Charsi and took her into their care. She has been a member of this organization ever since, using her immense physical strength to forge the order's weaponry and armor.

Covetous Shen

In recent years, I have heard rumors of a wandering jeweler who is currently searching for a gem known as the jewel of Dirgest. These tales refer to the individual as Covetous Shen, an elderly man hailing from the northern lands of Xiansai. What I find most perplexing is that a number of historical records—some of them from centuries ago—tell similar stories. Each account relates a wizened old man from Xiansai hunting for Dirgest's jewel.

Cydaea

It is said that Azmodan, the Lord of Sin, commands seven powerful lieutenants. Among them is Cydaea, the Maiden of Lust. Vizjerei writings depict her as Azmodan's favored servant, a demoness who is both exquisitely beautiful and nightmarish to behold. She inhabits the Lord of Sin's pleasure palace, reveling in blurring the lines between pleasure and pain, ecstasy and utter torment.

Emperor Hakan II

Born to an impoverished family in the far north, the young boy
Hakan II now sits on the throne as emperor of Kehjistan.
You may ask yourself how someone from such a low social

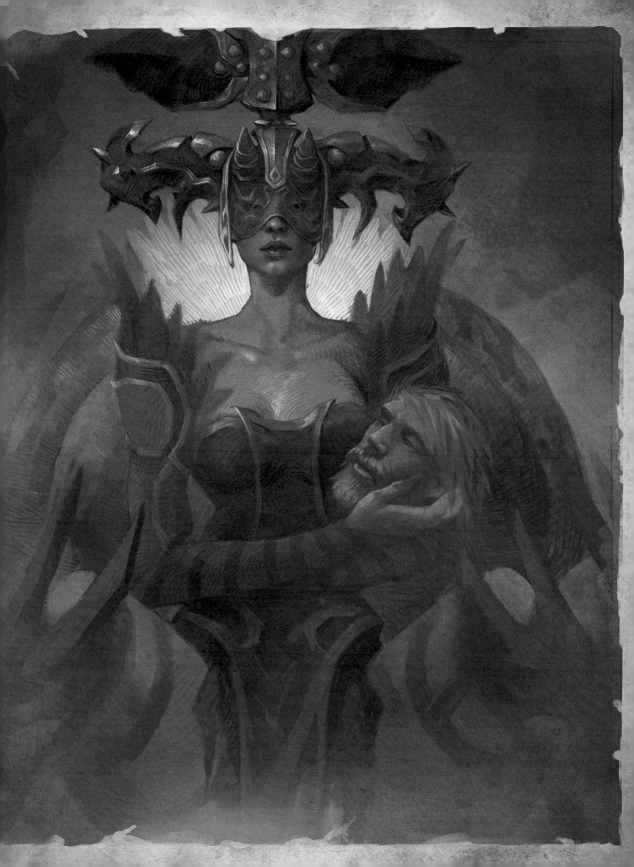

standing attained such a lofty position. The answer lies with the Zakarum. For some time, the priesthood has held power over deciding the empire's succession of rulers. Through a series of secret rituals, the members of the church discovered Hakan II's presence in the north and determined that he would become Kehjistan's newest emperor.

Belial later possessed Hakan II. He used the boy to sow chaos in Caldeum before my allies vanquished him.

Emperor Tassara (deceased)

Tassara lived in a time when wealth, power, and blood determined who would reign over Kehjistan. As such, he was carefully groomed for the position of emperor from childhood. He studied the intricacies of history and politics, all the while learning from the mistakes of his predecessors. Indeed, it can be said he was one of Kehjistan's greatest rulers. Tassara initiated many reforms in his day, such as making Zakarum the empire's official religion. For that act alone, he is revered by the church.

Fara

Fara was once a devout paladin of the Zakarum. Upon discovering that evil had taken root in the church, she abandoned her order and settled in Lut Gholein. I met her there, toiling under the scorching desert sun as a blacksmith. Despite this drastic change in lifestyle, Fara still holds fast to the teachings of the Zakarum founder, Akarat, believing they are pure and noble regardless of the church's corruption.

Farnham (deceased)

I remember Farnham in his better days—a jovial and well-spirited resident of Tristram. When King Leoric's youngest son, Prince Albrecht, went missing, Lazarus rallied Farnham and many other residents to venture into the cursed depths of the town's cathedral and rescue the boy. Although Farnham returned with his life, he left his sanity and will to live behind. Up until the day of his death at the hands of marauding demons, he slipped further into despair, finding solace only in heavy drinking.

Garreth Rau (deceased)

Garreth Rau was a brilliant scholar and one of the finest bookmakers in all of Sanctuary. He possessed

Covetous Shen

Hephasto the Armorer

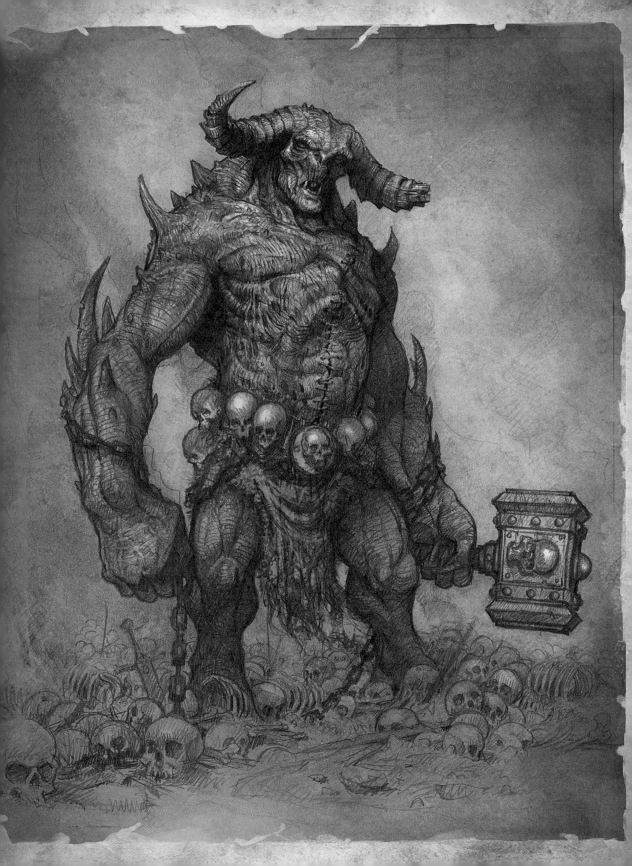

a natural affinity to magic, one he honed under the tutelage of a Taan mage. Later in life, Rau led the First Ones, a group of young and valiant scholars who dedicated themselves to carrying on the teachings of the original Horadrim.

At some point before these events, Belial took great interest in Rau and his abilities. He shrouded the man's thoughts and memories in a veil of lies, molding him into a puppet. Fueled by Belial's dark will, Rau conquered Gea Kul in the hopes of awakening an army of ancient sorcerers buried beneath the city.

I worked to thwart Rau's plans with a handful of brave individuals (even Leah was by my side at the time), but his powers proved too great for us to stand against. In the end, whatever humanity was left in Rau clawed its way through Belial's deception. Seeing the twisted pawn of evil he had become, the former scholar chose to take his own life.

Gharbad (deceased)

Most people consider khazra nothing more than mindless beasts, but they can be cunning and manipulative creatures. One of them, Gharbad, attempted to win the trust of Prince Aidan and his allies amid the Darkening of Tristram. Only later did the flea-bitten creature reveal his true murderous nature, for which he was slain.

Ghom

Ghom, the Lord of Gluttony, is one of Azmodan's seven loyal lieutenants. His appetite is insatiable, and he is known to consume his enemies as well as any demonic allies who stray too close to any of his slavering maws. Noxious filth oozes from his every pore, emitting a stench so powerful that it alone can choke the life from mortals.

Gillian

Gillian was the barmaid of Tristram's Tavern of the Rising Sun. Her smile and kind words could brighten the day of the most sullen patrons. After the Darkening of Tristram, the witch Adria invited her to the famed city of Caldeum. The barmaid seized the opportunity to leave her ravaged home behind and start life anew.

In Caldeum, Adria gave birth to Leah and left the infant in Gillian's care. Thereafter, the witch disappeared, never to return. The years that followed were hard on Gillian. When I finally met

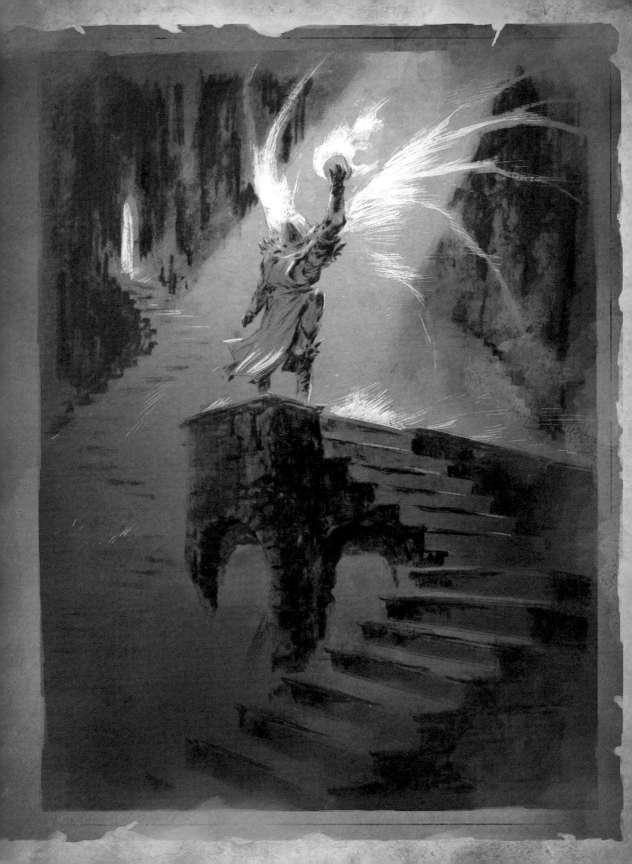

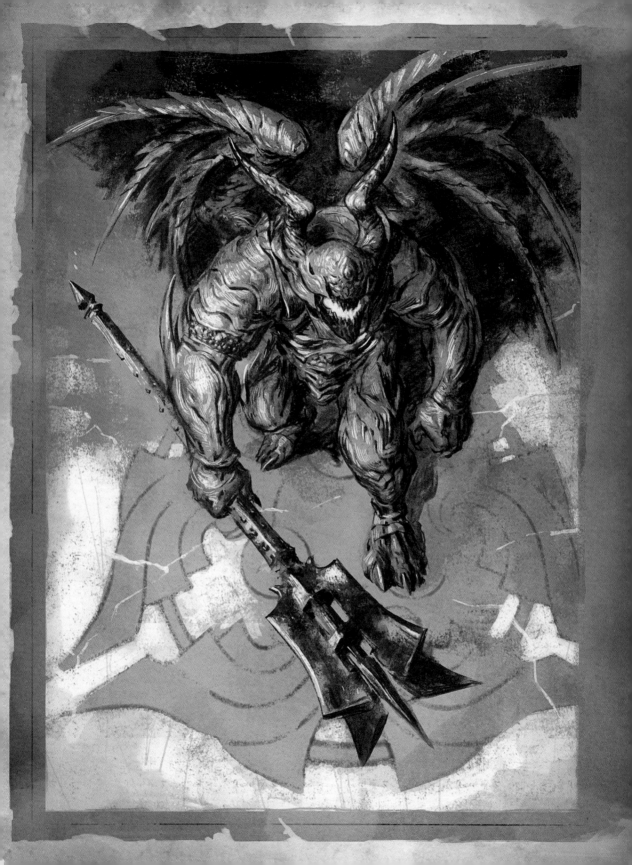

with her some years later, she was a different person. She was hollow. Cold. Distant. Dark voices had peeled away at her sanity, and she saw Leah as a dire threat.

Gripped in the throes of madness, Gillian attempted to murder Leah and me by burning down her home in the night. Fortunately, all of us escaped the flames unscathed. After this event, I took Leah into my care. I am sad to say that Gillian was beyond my saving. City guards locked her away in one of Caldeum's madhouses.

Griswold (deceased)

Griswold came to Tristram a number of years before Diablo's release, seeking a new place to ply his blacksmithing trade. When the Lord of Terror's shadow fell over the town, the burly man suffered a terrible wound while battling the demons beneath the cathedral, leaving him incapable of fighting. Even so, Griswold did what he could to help Prince Aidan and his allies scour evil from Tristram. In the end, the minions of the Hells slew the blacksmith and transformed him into a murderous undead terror.

Cain's theories concerning my relationship to Hadriel as well as the angel's decision to aid the mortal champions are correct.

Hadriel

When my companions ventured into the Burning Hells to destroy the soulstone of Mephisto and slay Diablo, they claimed that an angel named Hadriel aided them. Who was this figure? Why did he appear in the Hells? Personally, I believe Hadriel was a follower of Tyrael, specifically one who had learned of the archangel's involvement with Sanctuary. Following this discovery, he came of his own volition to help my allies traverse the perilous and twisting pathways of the Hells. This, however, is mere speculation on my part, for I have heard no other mention of Hadriel in recent years.

Haedrig Eamon

I have found the blacksmith Haedrig Eamon a warm and cheery fellow. He reminds me somewhat of his grandfather, Chancellor Eamon, a man who served King Leoric amid the Darkening of Tristram. I should note, however, that Haedrig was in Caldeum during that horrific period of history. Only much later did he come to Khanduras and settle in New Tristram with his wife and a promising apprentice. I am always surprised at the level of care and detail he puts into his blacksmithing work, even for menial tasks. Indeed, he is a man of great talent with a bright future ahead of him.

Hephasto the Armorer

Hephasto is a paradox of the Burning Hells. The hulking demon is a minion of Baal, and thus is driven by an overriding desire to destroy everything he touches. Yet at the same time, Hephasto possesses the ability to create. He toiled in the fiery Hellforge, molding incredible weapons to arm his demonic comrades for battle. I think, perhaps, he managed to channel his destructive nature, fusing it into the armaments he forged. It is even said the brute took great pride in the knowledge that his creations would cause untold death and carnage.

Nearly twenty years ago, a band of mortal champions struck Hephasto down while infiltrating the Hellforge. Some ancient Vizjerei texts claim that demons have the potential to be reborn in their desiccated realm after death. If this is true, I think it is possible the armorer of Hell will at some point in the future return.

Horazon

Horazon was a mage of the Vizjerei clan, perhaps one of the greatest who has ever lived. With regards to his philosophies about demons, he believed in breaking their wills and subjecting them to his complete dominance. Eventually, Horazon came to realize that the use of demons would bring about the downfall of all mankind.

Following the costly Mage Clan Wars (a subject I touch on in other places) and his terrible battle with Bartuc, Horazon disappeared from society, crafting a bastion called the Arcane Sanctuary, where he studied the secrets of the arcane. I do not know whether he is still alive, but considering the immense powers Horazon had at his command, I believe he might have found a means to prolong his life.

Iben Fahd (deceased)

Iben Fahd was a skilled Horadric mage who hailed from the Ammuit clan. He was one of the brave individuals who infiltrated Zoltun Kulle's archives and helped dismember the mad wizard. According to the Horadric texts, Iben was given the gruesome task of hiding away Kulle's head.

Khelric

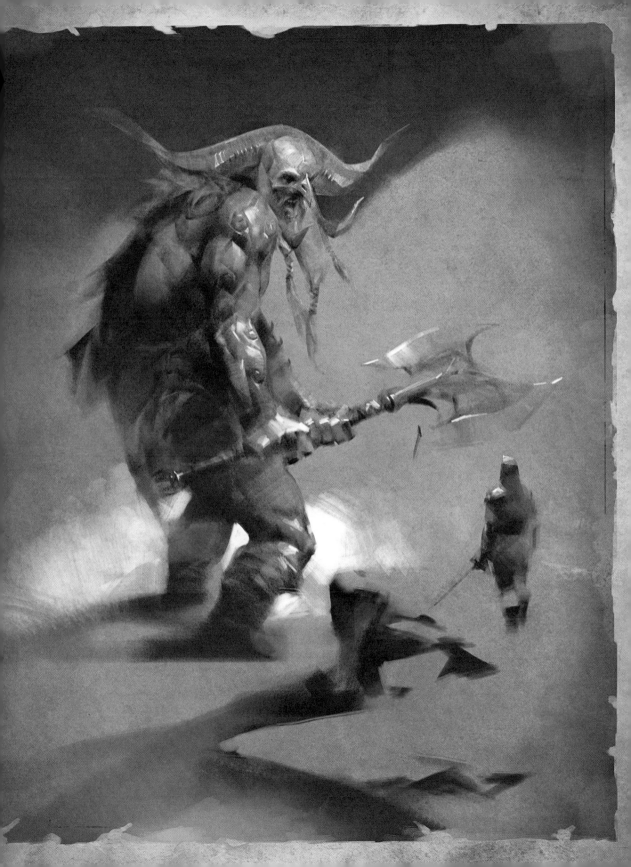

Izual

Izual did return, called to serve the Prime Evil. My allies defeated him in the High Heavens, where he and I had once walked together as great friends.

Let the tale of Izual stand as a reminder that even angels, the embodiments of order, can be twisted to chaos by the powers of the Burning Hells. . . .

A trusted lieutenant of Archangel Tyrael, Izual was captured during an assault on the Hells. Thereafter, the Prime Evils subjected the angel to horrific acts of torture. It is even said that Izual relinquished secrets regarding the soulstones to his demonic captors.

Nearly twenty years ago, when my mortal comrades forged into the Hells to do battle with Diablo, they struck down the corrupted Izual. However, I often wonder whether he will one day be reborn in the Hells, a cursed ability that other demons are rumored to possess.

Jacob Staalek

Jacob no longer carries El'druin. I summoned the Sword of Justice to my side after returning to the High Heavens.

In recent years, I have heard stories of an individual named Jacob, born and raised in the northern settlement of Staalbreak. The barbarian Owl tribe, infected by a demonic rage plague, repeatedly assaulted the town and spread corruption among its populace. As the story goes, Jacob was forced to slay his own father, who had succumbed to the terrible affliction. The young man was thereafter hunted for the crime of murder. Ultimately, he redeemed himself by vanquishing the foul demon responsible for the plague: Maluus.

What I find incredible about this tale is that, at some point, Jacob took up Tyrael's legendary Sword of Justice, El'druin. How did this come to pass? I can only assume that when Tyrael destroyed the Worldstone, his angelic blade was cast off and left unattended in the western lands. Whatever the case, clearly this man must possess a righteous heart to successfully wield El'druin.

Jazreth (deceased)

During the Darkening of Tristram, the Vizjerei mage Jazreth journeyed to my town, drawn by rumors of the demonic presence there. Battling Diablo's minions bled whatever valor and restraint had once existed in the man's heart. Calling himself the Summoner, he set out to find Horazon's legendary Arcane Sanctuary and pilfer its secrets for personal power. Fortunately, he perished while undergoing this quest.

Jered Cain (deceased)

Much of what I know concerning the Horadrim, demons, angels, and various arcana is due to the meticulous records handed down to me by Jered Cain. Oddly, I do not know very much concerning my ancestor's early life. He was a great Vizjerei mage—that much is irrefutable. Some accounts also say he was troubled by a terrible event in his past. What this was remains unclear, but I believe that through the Horadrim, Jered might have found a means to renew his purpose in life.

At Tyrael's behest, my ancestor and his comrades embarked on an arduous quest—the Hunt for the Three—to track down and imprison the Prime Evils. It was following the defeat of Mephisto and Baal that Jered became leader of the Horadrim. With wisdom and unyielding determination, he led his fellow mages in a horrific battle against Diablo—a battle that ended with the Prime Evil's capture in the Crimson Soulstone. It appears that Jered spent the rest of his days living in the Horadric monastery near what would become Tristram.

Karybdus

Necromancers consider themselves the keepers of the Balance between the forces of the Burning Hells and the High Heavens. However, I have heard tales that one member of this order, Karybdus, went to dangerous extremes to pursue this ideal. Indeed, it is said he summoned the demon Astrogha into Sanctuary, although it is difficult to understand what motives—however noble—would drive him to commit such a heinous act.

It appears that Karybdus's fellow necromancers also viewed his choices as disastrous. One of them, a man by the name of Zayl, eventually imprisoned both Karybdus and Astrogha in a strange artifact known as the Moon of the Spider.

Kashya

Kashya commands the martial forces of the Sisters of the Sightless Eye. I have witnessed her prowess myself and consider her one of the greatest archers the order has ever produced. In addition, I know Kashya to possess an unequalled genius in strategic and tactical matters.

Kehr

Ever since the destruction of Mount Arreat, the barbarians have been a troubled and wayfaring people. There are many, however, who still strive to live with purpose and honor. I know the man named Kehr to be one of them. He stands watch over the Iron Path, a mountain road north of Khanduras plagued by khazra attacks. Under Kehr's unwavering vigilance, the route has become a safe passage for all travelers.

Khelric (deceased)

Khelric was the mighty barbarian chief of the Owl tribe. At some point (and the sources differ on when) the demon Maluus possessed this proud warrior and used him to spread a vile demonic rage plague. A young man named Jacob Staalek, armed with Archangel Tyrael's Sword of Justice, ultimately vanquished Khelric in single combat. By that time, Maluus had warped the barbarian chief's body into a horrific seething vessel of pure hatred.

Korsikk (deceased)

Korsikk was the son of Rakkis and the second king of Westmarch. During his reign, he ordered the construction of the great Bastion's Keep as a means to thwart barbarian aggression in the north. Korsikk later gathered his forces and boldly set out to do what even his father could not: crush the barbarian tribes once and for all. It is said that the king died an ignoble death on this campaign, struck down by his hated foes.

Lachdanan (deceased)

I remember Lachdanan with fondness. He was a righteous man, captain of King Leoric's army. When Tristram's monarch succumbed to Diablo's influence, Lachdanan slew his liege, seeing no other means to spare the town from the rising tide of darkness.

    The captain and his closest allies buried the king beneath Tristram's cathedral, but what happened next is something of a mystery. It is said Leoric rose from the dead as the Skeleton King and cursed Lachdanan and his comrades. Thereafter, the captain resolved to wander the cathedral's subterranean catacombs to the end of his days rather than spread the evil that gnawed at his heart among the innocent townsfolk of Tristram.

Lazarus (deceased)

There are times when I awake in the dead of night plagued by nightmares of Lazarus. What can I say of this despicable man? He was an archbishop of the Zakarum Church, and I believe he was one of the first members of the faith to be irrevocably corrupted by the Prime Evils. Lazarus was a great orator, and he used this skill to win Leoric's trust. Indeed, the archbishop was instrumental in convincing the man to undertake the journey to Tristram and proclaim himself the king of Khanduras.

    Once in Tristram, Lazarus released Diablo from his Crimson Soulstone, setting into motion a chain of events that would lead to the deaths of countless innocents. Prince Aidan later struck

Mikulov

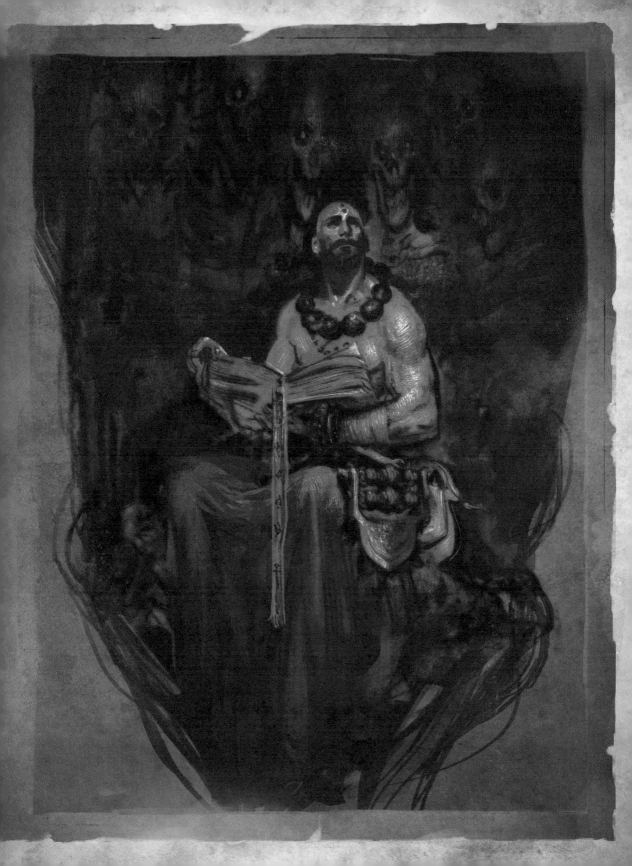

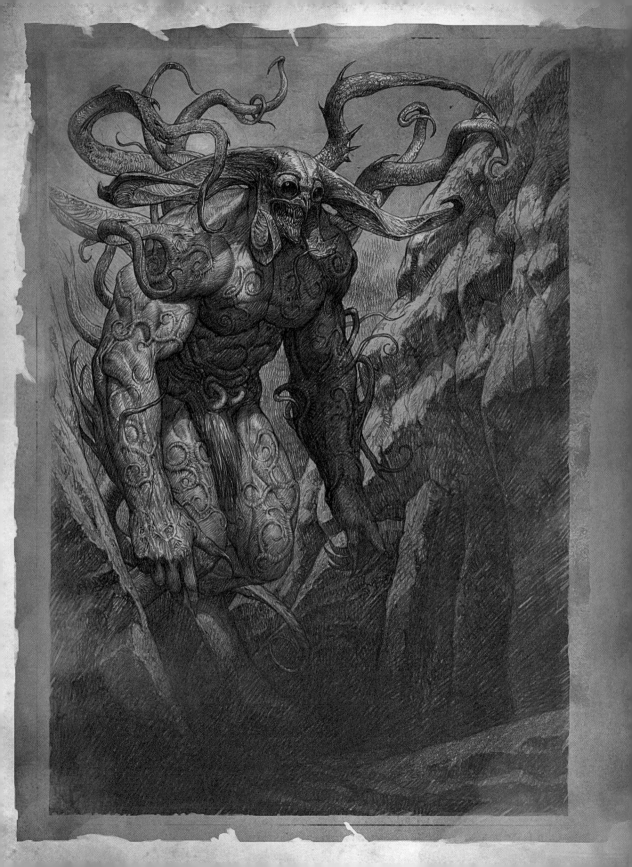

down the archbishop, but to this day I wonder how many lives I could have saved if I had seen through Lazarus's guise of benevolence and wisdom.

Li-Ming

Every so often, I hear of a promising new student accepted into Caldeum's Yshari Sanctum. Li-Ming, a young woman from Xiansai, is perhaps the most recent of these individuals. She is said to possess an almost insatiable appetite for arcane knowledge and an incredible affinity to magic. I only hope that, as the years wear on, she also learns to use her vast powers with restraint and wisdom.

Lucion

Lucion is the ill-begotten son of Mephisto. Unlike his sister, Lilith, he served his father without question (or, at least, he appeared to do so). At the behest of the Prime Evils, Lucion came to the world of Sanctuary and forged the Triune, a seemingly benevolent cult that, in reality, aimed to turn the hearts of mankind to darkness. Mephisto's son then took on the role of the cult's spiritual leader, calling himself the Primus.

It should be noted that Lucion assumed a mortal guise for this task. Indeed, the *Books of Kalan* describe him as a charismatic and wise man with a voice so soothing it bordered on the hypnotic. Only later, when the nephalem Uldyssian ul-Diomed and his followers assaulted the Triune, did Lucion reveal his true demonic form. Yet even the demon's immense powers could not withstand the might of the nephalem army.

Maghda

A storm of dark rumors and lies swirls around Maghda and her origins. I know she is practiced in the arts of witchcraft, and I know also that she leads the Coven, a cult that has carried on the traditions of the Triune. There is nothing she would not do—no one she would not sacrifice—to appease the Lords of the Burning Hells. Beyond these unsettling facts, the woman's past remains a mystery.

Malus

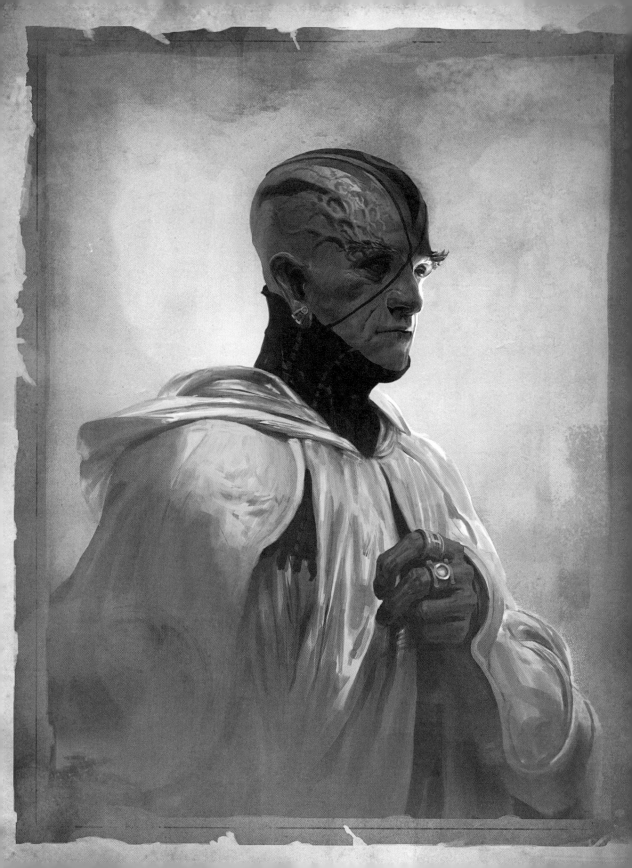

Malic (deceased)

During the era of the Sin War, the human Malic fell under the sway of the Prime Evils. He became a loyal member of the Triune, rising to the lofty position of high priest. For his dedication, the Lords of the Burning Hells granted Malic unnatural longevity and other gifts. The *Books of Kalan* state that, outwardly, he was a handsome and physically intimidating man. But beneath this facade, Malic was withered and grotesque.

Amid the Sin War, he was flayed alive by the demoness Lilith, who had manipulated the nephalem in the guise of a mortal named Lylia. I find Malic's fate a fitting end to a man who shrouded himself in a veil of lies to deceive so many innocent people.

Maluus

I consider Maluus to be a servant of Mephisto, but this is something of conjecture on my part. What I know, however, is that the demon came to the world of Sanctuary sometime after the Darkening of Tristram and spread a plague among the barbarian tribes. It is said that merely touching Maluus's blood was enough to blind a mortal with murderous rage. A young human named Jacob Staalek ultimately vanquished the demon, casting the creature and the foul plague back into the roiling pits of the Hells.

Mendeln

Mendeln was the brother of Uldyssian ul-Diomed. According to one account I have found, he befriended the legendary nephalem Rathma and, through this wise being's teachings, became a necromancer. Recently, I made a startling discovery concerning this man—he was also known as Kalan, the enigmatic figure who authored the *Books of Kalan*. I do not know when this change in name occurred, or the reasons for it. I am, however, in debt to Mendeln for the knowledge he has passed down through his tomes.

Mikulov

I met Mikulov during my investigation of Garreth Rau and the First Ones (a subject I have written on elsewhere). This brave man is one of Ivgorod's monks, a spiritual warrior molded into a living weapon through years of harsh and unrelenting training. During the course of his studies, Mikulov learned of a prophecy that stated the Horadrim would play a vital role in an impending battle— one that would pit the living against the dead. This chilling discovery spurred the monk to seek me out, for he believed that I had some part to play in forestalling this dark fate.

The simple truth, however, is that Mikulov did far more to spare the world from this prophecy than me. Without this fearless monk at my side, both Leah and I would have perished at the hands of Rau and his barbarous servants. I owe Mikulov my life, and I hope that a day may come when I can repay the debt.

Morbed

Recently, I learned of a man named Morbed, a former thief said to have a mysterious lantern (one, I might add, that he keeps shackled to his wrist). It is said this individual can wield abilities possessed by necromancers, wizards, crusaders, and even druids. I find it hard to believe that one man could have command over such diverse forms of magic, but I do not question that Morbed exists. Indeed, I have heard a number of tales about him wandering the lands of Sanctuary, lending aid to those in need. As to his motivations, it seems he helps others as atonement for some terrible sin in his past.

Moreina (deceased)

Amid the Darkening of Tristram, a cowled and shadowy figure arrived in the town to battle the forces of the Burning Hells. Her name was Moreina, and she was one of the highly skilled rogues from the Sisters of the Sightless Eye. When at last evil had been purged from Tristram, this brave woman ventured back to her order. But she carried something dark with her—a silent madness that ate away at her once noble heart. Assuming the name Blood Raven, she fell into league with the Lesser Evil Andariel and assaulted her fellow rogues before finally being killed.

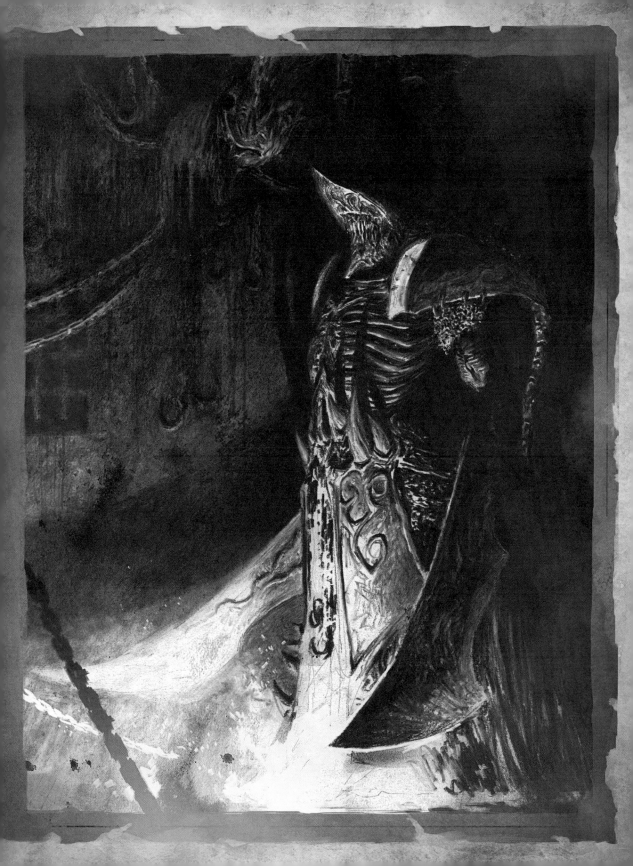

Natalya

Natalya once belonged to the Viz-Jaq'taar, the shadowy group of assassins tasked with hunting down renegade mages. In recent years, it appears that she has abandoned her order to take up the cause of the demon hunters, a cadre of warriors dedicated to eradicating the minions of the Burning Hells from the lands of Sanctuary.

Nihlathak (deceased)

Nihlathak was a respected figure among the barbarians and a member of the Council of Elders. When Baal began his bloody march toward Mount Arreat, this circle of venerated leaders gathered to decide on what course of action to take. They chose to cast an ancient and dangerous warding spell that would shield the town of Harrogath, the last settlement that stood between Baal and the summit of Arreat. All members of the council died during this selfless act.

All, that is, except Nihlathak.

Over the course of Baal's march through barbarian lands, Nihlathak had grown increasingly distressed. He had watched his people die, watched his lands be irrevocably tainted by the marauding armies of the Hells. Ultimately, he believed that only by making a pact with Baal could the barbarians survive the ordeal. So it was that Nihlathak gave Baal the Relic of the Ancients, a legendary artifact needed to bypass Arreat's defenses and reach the summit, in exchange for sparing the town of Harrogath.

Although his motivations may seem noble, the fact is that through this act, Nihlathak allowed Baal to corrupt the Worldstone, setting off a chain of events that would end with Arreat's destruction. Nihlathak himself, twisted by evil after forging his foul agreement with Baal, met his end before the mountain was destroyed.

Nor Tiraj (deceased)

The Vizjerei mage Nor Tiraj was one of the most prolific scholars of the Horadrim. He is referred to as an acolyte in many places, which leads me to believe that he was not one of the original members of the order. From what I have gathered, he remained in Khanduras following the Hunt for the Three, living out his days by adding to the region's great Horadric library alongside my ancestor Jered Cain.

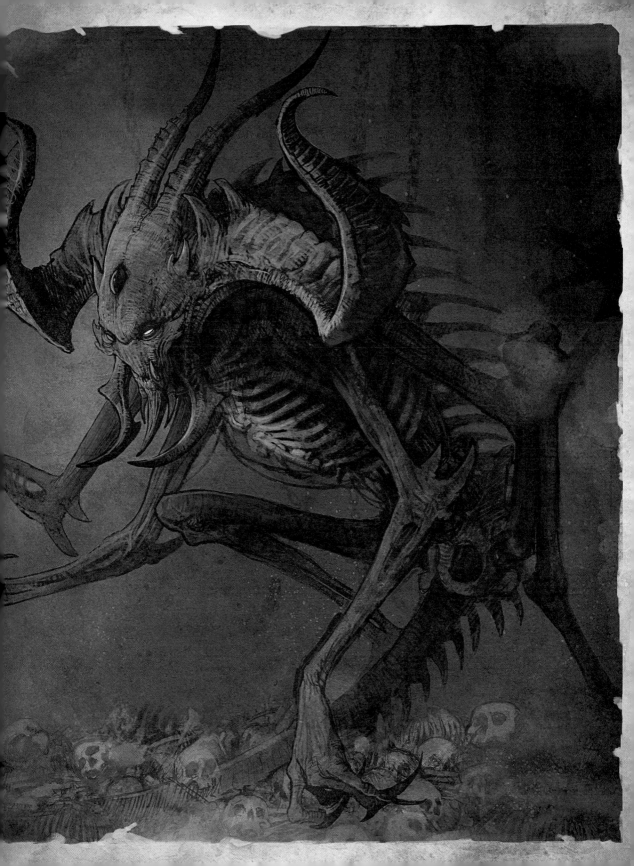

Norrec Vizharan

I first learned of the treasure seeker and soldier-for-hire Norrec Vizharan during a trip to the city of Westmarch. There, a fellow scholar related the man's story. Vizharan, under the employ of a Vizjerei mage, apparently stumbled across the cursed armor of Bartuc, the Warlord of Blood. Upon donning the pieces, the treasure seeker was overcome with a lust for death, and he turned against his own companions. I do not know how many people Vizharan killed while struggling against the armor's malevolent influence, but my colleague claims that he eventually managed to free himself from the curse.

Ogden (deceased)

Ogden was the proprietor of Tristram's Tavern of the Rising Sun, a warmhearted man whom nearly all of the town's populace considered a friend. Tragically, both he and his loving wife, Garda, perished while trying to save others from a wave of demons that descended on Tristram.

Ord Rekar (deceased)

Ord Rekar was a proud and respected member of the barbarian Council of Elders. I considered him the foundation of the organization, the embodiment of its wisdom and strength. Rekar gave his own life when he and his comrades cast the great warding spell to protect Harrogath from the advancing demonic armies of Baal.

Ormus

I met Ormus on the docks of Kurast nearly twenty years ago. He had a strange manner of speaking, one that my own comrades attributed to insanity. I, however, suspect that Ormus is a wise and incredibly gifted mage. His spellwork revealed him to be a member of the Taan clan, which focuses on the use of divination, scrying, and other abilities rooted in old Skatsimi mystical rites.

Pepin (deceased)

Pepin was one of my closest friends in Tristram. He was a caring man who had long studied the arts of medicine and healing. He put these skills to great use amid the Darkening of Tristram, saving many lives. I later witnessed Pepin's death at the hands of demons. I will not repeat the horrific details here. Suffice it to say the images are branded into my mind, and I fear they will haunt me until the end of my days.

Pindleskin (deceased)

I first heard of the skeletal terror Pindleskin during Baal's assault against Mount Arreat. Since then, I have struggled to find details concerning what this creature was. The account I find most interesting relates to a famous barbarian chief. Centuries ago, the Kehjistani general Rakkis invaded the lands surrounding Mount Arreat. His armies clashed with the barbarian tribes and were turned back, but not before inflicting considerable damage. The chief of the Bear tribe—a man of incredible physical strength—was one of the victims. I believe Pindleskin was the remains of this mighty barbarian leader, pulled from the grave by the foul magic that pervaded Baal's armies.

Quov Tsin (presumed deceased)

Quov Tsin was a mage of the Vizjerei clan who sought out the legendary city of Ureh. Incredibly, it appears he found this location and met with its reclusive ruler, an individual named Juris Khan. There is no mention, however, of Quov ever returning from his journey. As such, I assume that at some point he perished in the fabled halls of Ureh.

Rakanishu

The fallen are despicable and violent creatures driven by wanton destruction. According to Vizjerei accounts (and my observations), they rarely ever travel alone. They are pack creatures, and as such, certain fallen inevitably rise to dominant positions among their respective groups. Perhaps the most famous is Rakanishu, a particularly brutal fallen who is feared and respected even by his own barbaric kind.

As with Izual, the Prime Evil summoned Rakanoth to his side during the assault on the High Heavens.

Rakanoth, the Lord of Despair

The demon Rakanoth is a master of torture who once ruled over the Plains of Despair in the Burning Hells. It is said he served Andariel, the Maiden of Anguish, before shifting allegiances (but whom he answers to now remains a mystery). Certain Vizjerei tomes state that Rakanoth was the warden of the captive angel Izual. For many long years, he subjected his prisoner to excruciating and otherworldly forms of torture.

Rumford

The tireless farmer Rumford is one of the many respectable individuals I have met in New Tristram. He seems a humble and introverted man, but I think there is more to him than that. I have heard that his ancestor was one of Rakkis's most loyal lieutenants, a charismatic soldier who eventually settled in Khanduras. Due to this lineage, I believe the blood of a leader runs through Rumford's veins, whether he realizes it or not.

When I fell to Sanctuary and the dead rose from their graves, Rumford valiantly sacrificed his own life to protect the people of New Tristram.

Sankekur (deceased)

Sankekur occupied the seat of the Que-Hegan, the highest divine authority of the Zakarum Church. As such, it is safe to say he was once the most powerful living mortal in all of Sanctuary. Thousands of fanatical worshippers answered to his every beck and call. At some point during his reign, Sankekur succumbed to the influence of Mephisto. The Lord of Hatred later overtook the Que-Hegan completely, twisting the man's body into a horrific demonic visage.

Shanar

Shanar is one of the rebellious students of arcane magic known as wizards. I first heard her name through the stories of Jacob Staalek (whom I write on elsewhere). It appears that at one time, she set out to study the nature of the Crystal Arch and the presence of angelic resonances on Sanctuary. Her investigations ultimately led her to the resting place of Tyrael's lost sword, El'druin. The energies pervading the fabled artifact imprisoned her until Jacob finally arrived to take up the blade. Thereafter, the wizard allied with the young man, but I know nothing concerning her motivations for doing so, or whether she has continued her studies of the Crystal Arch.

Tal Rasha (deceased)

As with my ancestor Jered Cain, details concerning Tal Rasha's origins are somewhat difficult to come by. Many accounts of his life exist, but what am I to take for fact? In some cases, he is described as an Ammuit mage, one of the clan's greatest masters of illusion. Other accounts state he was Vizjerei or even Taan. What is irrefutable, however, is that he was a valorous man, which is perhaps why Archangel Tyrael chose him to lead the Horadrim during the Hunt for the Three.

Tal Rasha proved his bravery when the order clashed with Baal in the deserts of Aranoch. Amid the battle, the Lord of Destruction's Amber Soulstone was shattered. Selflessly, Tal Rasha decided to use his own body as a means to contain the Lord of Destruction. At their leader's behest, the Horadrim imprisoned Baal in the largest shard of the crystal and then plunged it into Tal Rasha. Thereafter, the mages sealed him in a subterranean tomb beneath the shifting desert sands.

Nearly three centuries later, Diablo liberated Baal from his prison. At that time, I believe there was nothing truly left of Tal Rasha beyond the withered husk that had once been his body.

Valla

The demon hunters are a relatively new order, formed in the wake of Mount Arreat's destruction. Nonetheless, I have heard stories concerning a number of this organization's members and their noble quest to purge Sanctuary of demonic influence.

Recently, a traveler passing through New Tristram told me of one noteworthy demon hunter by the name of Valla, a Westmarch native. It appears the minions of the Burning Hells slew her family when she was only a child. This harrowing event changed her forever, driving her to seek vengeance against all demons. In one instance, she tracked down and vanquished an insidious creature that had twisted the thoughts of children, spurring them to murder their friends and family. It is said that during this encounter, Valla's mind briefly merged with her demonic foe. I cannot imagine what horrors she witnessed as a result, but the fact that she emerged victorious clearly illustrates her incredible resilience and aptitude for slaying the creatures of Hell.

Warriv

The caravan master Warriv has been to exotic locales that I have only read of in books. I had the opportunity to travel with him after the fall of Tristram, although we later went our separate ways. I often wonder how the years have treated him. I consider him a trustworthy ally, and I hope his travels one day lead him back to Khanduras so that we can meet and speak again.

Wirt (deceased)

Wirt was a well-mannered boy who lived with his mother, Canace, in Tristram. After
Diablo's release, demons abducted the child and dragged him into the charnel house beneath
the town's cathedral. The blacksmith Griswold risked his life to save Wirt, but not before
the boy's leg was devoured by Hell's minions. The child's demeanor darkened considerably
following that event. Like nearly all of Tristram's residents, young Wirt was later killed by a
throng of ravenous demons.

Xazax

Xazax is a cunning and manipulative demon who serves Belial, the Lord of Lies. It is said
that a wayward sorceress by the name of Galeona summoned the mantis-like fiend into
Sanctuary for one task: to retrieve the cursed armor of Bartuc, the Warlord of Blood.
Fortunately, I have not heard any accounts that Xazax succeeded in this dark quest or that
he still walks the mortal realm.

Zayl

By all accounts, the necromancer Zayl is an unwavering adherent to the philosophies of his
order, tirelessly working to ensure that the powers of neither the Hells nor the Heavens hold too
much sway over the mortal realm. It appears he is also a well-traveled and learned individual,
for stories tell of his exploits from the lost city of Ureh to the kingdom of Westmarch. In each of
these cases, it seems he has worked to thwart the efforts of persons delving into demonic—
or other dark—arts.

    It is said that Zayl possesses a number of strange and powerful artifacts. Among them is a
skull, to which is bound the spirit of a mercenary named Humbart Wessel. Communing with
spirits is a common practice among necromancers, but usually these interactions are short-lived.
I find it interesting that Zayl keeps the skull and its spirit among his possessions.

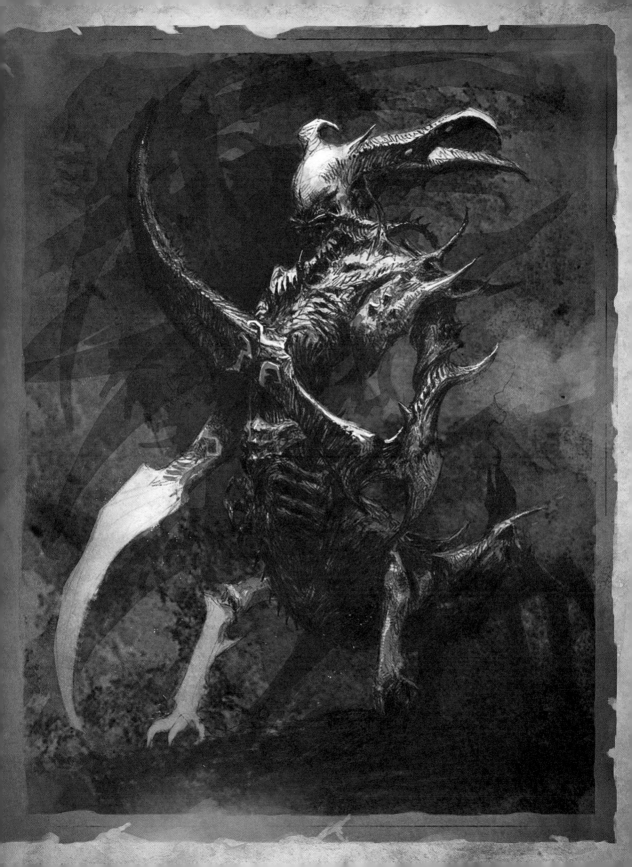

Zebulon I (deceased)

Zebulon I was one of the great Que-Hegans of Zakarum history. He initiated a set of sweeping reforms that leeched away some of the church's immense power and gave more freedom of worship to the common folk of Kehjistan. According to some historical accounts, Zebulon's decision came about after he received visions from Akarat, the legendary founder of the Zakarum faith.

Zhota

Mikulov spoke to me of how Ivgorod's holy warriors, the monks, each hold a certain god as his or her patron. He was especially fascinated by one of the order's youngest members, Zhota, who aligned himself with Ymil, the god of the rivers, emblematic of emotion, intuition, and life-giving properties. It appears this decision is somewhat rare among the monks, many of whom prize the strength and resolve attributed to deities such as Zaim, the god of the mountains, and Ytar, the god of fire.

I would not, however, attribute Zhota's choice to weakness by any stretch of the imagination. I have recently come to learn that his master is a man named Akyev the Unyielding. By all accounts, he is one of the strictest and most unforgiving monks in Ivgorod. Many initiates have been gravely injured (and, according to some rumors, even died) due to his brutal training methods. For Zhota to have endured all of his master's tests leads me to believe he is an incredibly resourceful and resilient individual.

Zayl

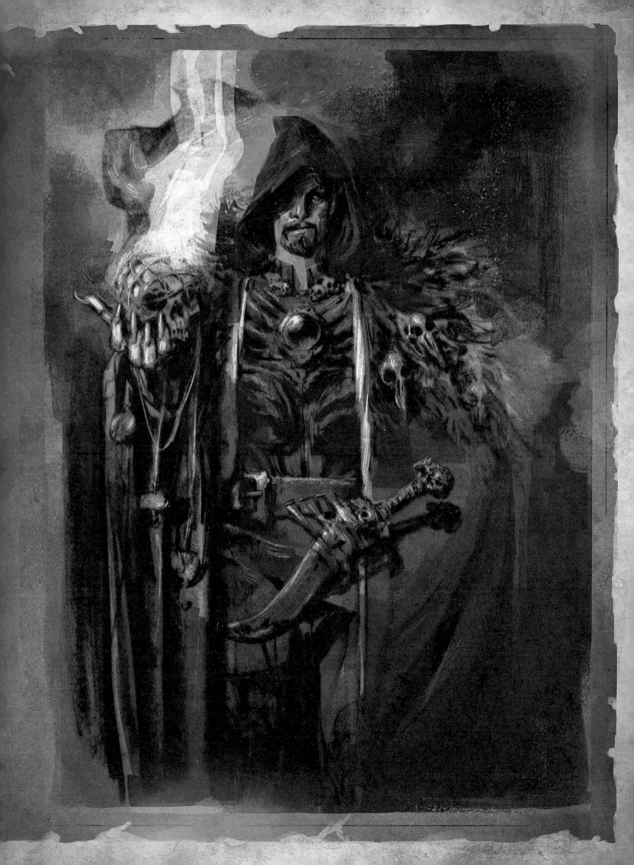

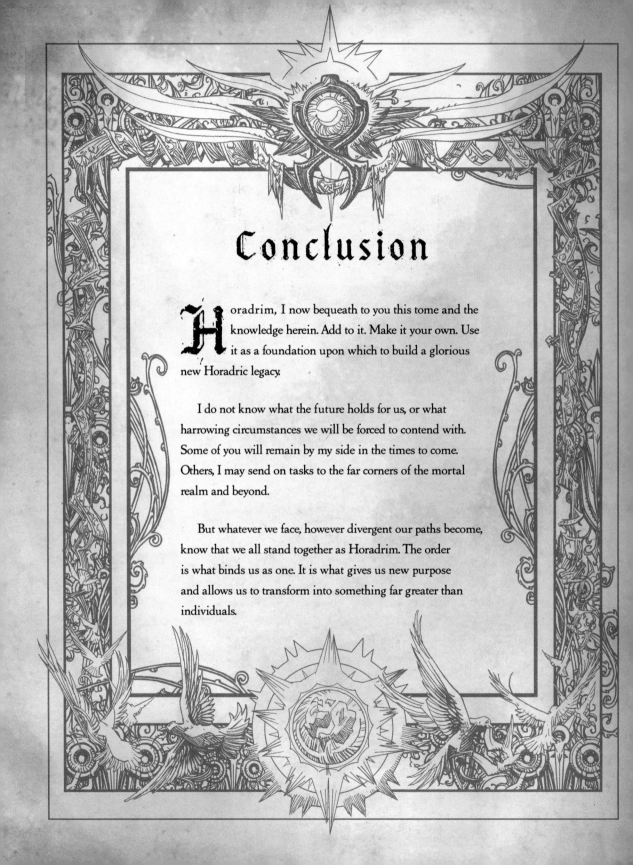

Conclusion

Horadrim, I now bequeath to you this tome and the knowledge herein. Add to it. Make it your own. Use it as a foundation upon which to build a glorious new Horadric legacy.

I do not know what the future holds for us, or what harrowing circumstances we will be forced to contend with. Some of you will remain by my side in the times to come. Others, I may send on tasks to the far corners of the mortal realm and beyond.

But whatever we face, however divergent our paths become, know that we all stand together as Horadrim. The order is what binds us as one. It is what gives us new purpose and allows us to transform into something far greater than individuals.

We are mortal, our lives brief flashes of light in the span of eternity. But through the Horadric knowledge we pass on, through the choices we make to uphold the order's tenets, we may transcend the ephemeral nature of our existence. We may become beacons of hope and courage that continue burning long after we leave this world.

Tal Rasha, Jered Cain, and the original Horadrim knew this. Deckard and Leah knew this. Although they are gone, who among you does not still look to them for guidance? Who among you does not find pride in the sacrifices they made and the valorous acts they performed? They live on through us, unfettered by the limitations of mortality.

In each and every one of your hearts is the same power—the same potential—that elevated these heroes to greatness. Find that place. Wield it as a light to guide you through the dark days that may lie ahead.

And remember always that whatever comes to pass, I will stand with you.

—Tyrael

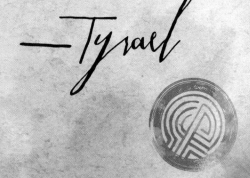

INSIGHT EDITIONS

PO BOX 3088
SAN RAFAEL, CA 94912
WWW.INSIGHTEDITIONS.COM

Originally published in 2013, and subsequently in paperback, by
Insight Editions, San Rafael, California, in 2016.

Library of Congress Cataloging-in-Publication Data available.

ISBN: 978-1-60887-803-1

REPLANTED PAPER   Insight Editions, in association with Roots
of Peace, will plant two trees for each tree used in the manufacturing of this
book. Roots of Peace is an internationally renowned humanitarian organization
dedicated to eradicating land mines worldwide and converting war-torn lands into
productive farms and wildlife habitats. Together, we will plant two million fruit
and nut trees in Afghanistan and provide farmers there with the skills and support
necessary for sustainable land use.

Manufactured in China

10 9 8 7 6 5 4 3 2 1

LICENSED BLIZZARD ENTERTAINMENT PRODUCT

BLIZZARD ENTERTAINMENT

Writings: Matt Burns

Creative Direction, Layout, and Design: Doug Alexander

Additional Story Development: Chris Metzen,
Micky Neilson, Brian Kindregan

Additional Art: Victor Lee

Producers: Josh Horst, Kyle Williams, Skye Chandler

Editor: Cate Gary

Lore: Justin Parker

Licensing: Matthew Beecher, Byron Parnell

Special Thanks: Christian Lichtner, John Polidora, David Lomeli,
Benjamin Zhang, Peter C. Lee, Leonard Boyarsky, Michael Chu,
Valerie Watrous, Evelyn Fredericksen, Sean Copeland,
Leanne Huynh, Audrey Vicenzi, Joseph Lacroix

INSIGHT EDITIONS

Publisher: Raoul Goff

Art Director: Chrissy Kwasnik

Executive Editor: Vanessa Lopez

Production Manager: Anna Wan

Editorial Assistant: Elaine Ou

ART CREDITS

The Black Frog—Pages 30, 61, 67, 137, 138, 145, 161

Nicolas Delort—Pages 50, 55, 57, 59, 64, 116, 125

ENrang—Pages 22, 27, 102-103, 122, 128, 148

Riccardo Federici—Pages 111, 131, 146

Gino—Pages 35, 43, 70-71, 76-77, 108-109

John Howe—Pages 38, 41

Joseph Lacroix—Pages 1, 2, 5, 6, 7, 8, 10, 11, 13, 18, 23, 26,
    37, 40, 42, 44, 45, 46, 47, 48, 49, 51, 52, 62, 63, 80, 102-103
    (background), 114-115 (background), 162, 163, 165, endpapers,
    bellyband, envelope (exterior and interior)

Iain McCaig—Pages 88-89, 96-97

Jon McConnell—Pages 69, 109 (top and bottom), 110, 112 (top),
    113 (left), 114 (center), 115 (top, left, and right), 117, 118, 119,
    120, 121, 123, 124, 126, 127

Petar Meseldzija—Pages 12, 19, 100, 105, Red Tree of Khanduras

Jean-Baptiste Monge—Pages 15, 16, 81, 93, 106, 112 (left),
    113 (right), 134, 135, 152-153

Glenn Rane—Cover

Ruan Jia—Page 9

Dan Hee Ryu—Pages 20, 21, 24, 25, 29, 32, 33, 34, 36,
    72, 73, 74, 75

Adrian Smith—Pages 82-83, 84-85, 86-87, 90-91, 99,
    151, 156, 159

Yang Qi—Pages 94-95

Bin Zhang—Pages 132-133

Zhang Lu—Pages 140-141